BETH'S LITTLE

Riverbend, Texas Heat 2

Marla Monroe

MENAGE EVERLASTING

Siren Publishing, Inc.
www.SirenPublishing.com

A SIREN PUBLISHING BOOK
IMPRINT: Ménage Everlasting

BETH'S LITTLE SECRET
Copyright © 2012 by Marla Monroe

ISBN: 978-1-62241-443-7

First Printing: October 2012

Cover design by Les Byerley
All art and logo copyright © 2012 by Siren Publishing, Inc.

PUBLISHER
Siren Publishing, Inc.
www.SirenPublishing.com

BETH'S LITTLE SECRET

Riverbend, Texas Heat 2

MARLA MONROE
Copyright © 2012

Chapter One

Sheriff Mac Tidwell pulled in behind Bethany Hallmark's Nissan Pathfinder and cut the engine. She had called about a Peeping Tom complaint a week ago, and now she was calling in that someone had left something on her porch. He steeled himself to see her again. He and his brother, Mason, had been fighting their attraction to the pretty, sable-haired beauty for years now. They didn't think she was up for their sort of games.

Now, he was forced to spend time with her again. His cock jerked behind the zipper of his uniform pants. He adjusted it before he got out of the truck. Then he walked up to the front porch and looked at the basket sitting at her front door. Before he could take another step, the door opened, and Beth peered out at him from behind her reading glasses. Her pretty hazel eyes looked more amber today than usual.

"Beth, how are you doing?"

"Okay. I want that off my porch." She nodded toward the basket he had yet to see inside.

"All right, let me take a look."

"Can't you just take it away and look at it later?" she asked.

"I need to see it like you found it. Did you look at it from where you are now or from the other side?"

"I found it when I got home from the store. I was standing right in front of it." She pointed toward the porch directly in front of him.

Mac nodded and walked up on the porch to where she had pointed. He pulled off his sunglasses and stuck them in his front shirt pocket before bending over and lifting up the towel that covered the basket.

Inside the basket lay a pair of handcuffs, a feather, and a candle. The note lying on top said, *You're my favorite one. I'll give you everything you want. Wait for me.*

"Do you know who sent this to you?" he asked, standing up straight again.

Beth looked up at him and shook her head *no*. "Not unless it's the same guy from last week."

"Do you know what he means in the note?"

"No."

"Do you know what the items in the basket are for?"

"No," she whispered.

Mac thought differently. She knew and wasn't telling. He didn't have to guess at their uses and thought about pressuring her. He decided against it for now. He needed to gather the evidence and go from there first.

"Okay, Beth. Go on back inside, and stay while I check everything out here. I'll knock when I need to talk to you again."

"Are you going to get rid of it?"

"I'm going to take it in as evidence, but other than trespassing, I don't know what kind of crime is being committed. I guess this could be a stalker, but this is the only evidence we have right now to go on."

"Please, just get rid of it." She leaned heavily on the door then closed it with a soft snap.

Mac sighed and walked back out to his truck for supplies. He would work it like a crime scene just in case. He didn't like the looks of the items in the basket. They were typical fetish items. The handcuffs worried him, though. They looked to be police grade at first glance. If Beth had picked up a stalker, he would put a stop to it right quick.

He didn't like the fact that she lived where she did, or that she lived alone, but there wasn't much he could do about it. She wasn't his to take care of. If she had been, she would have been living with him and Mason. There wouldn't be any chance of a stalker getting within ten feet of her. He drew in a deep breath and let it out. Time to get to work.

Thirty minutes later, he had everything he needed from the porch. He locked up his truck and knocked on Beth's door. She answered it after checking to see who it was from the window. *Good girl.*

"Sheriff."

"Beth, we know each other well enough for you to call me Mac." When she didn't say anything, he sighed. "Can I come in?"

She took a step back and let him in then closed the door. She turned around and leaned back against it, hugging herself.

"Let's sit down, Beth, and talk. I need to ask you some questions."

Beth's eyes widened for a second, and then she nodded and walked over to the couch where she sat down. He took a chair across from her and pulled out his note pad to write.

"Tell me about how you found it today. Where had you been?"

"I usually go to the store on Saturday for groceries. I left here about nine and got back around ten thirty. I had to stop by the post office first. I walked up on the porch with my hands full and just figured it was from someone I knew. I unlocked the door and took my groceries in then walked back out and got another load. When I finished putting everything perishable away, I went back out to get the basket. Something made me look at it before I picked it up. When I saw what was in it, I walked inside and closed the door and called the office."

"Did you touch anything inside the basket?"

"No! I only pulled back the towel then put it back and left it where it was."

Mac nodded. He didn't like asking these questions, but he had to.

"Do you have a boyfriend who might have brought this over as a joke or something?"

"No, I don't have a boyfriend."

"Who are the last couple of people you have dated?"

"What? Why do you need to know that?"

"It's just to rule out anyone playing a prank, Beth."

"I haven't dated anyone in over a year. I don't even remember who the last few were."

Mac's cock twitched at that bit of news. He hadn't realized she wasn't dating anyone. He'd worked hard to not know anything about her personal life.

"So, no bad breakups lately?"

"No."

"What about in the past, Beth? Even two or three years ago."

"I–I don't know. I'd have to think about it."

"Have you had any odd phone calls recently?"

"No."

"No hang-ups or wrong numbers?"

"No, I only have my cell phone, and no one has the number but a few close friends."

Mac knew he wasn't in that *close friend* category, but he had her number now.

"Do you have a security system, Beth?"

"No, I've never needed one. I have good locks, deadbolts."

"You might want to think about a security system. You're a young woman living alone. Even if this ends up just being a prank, it would be safer for you living outside of town like you do."

"I–I'll think about it."

He stood up and closed his pad. "Okay, I'm going to walk around the house and see if there is anything out of the ordinary. Then I'll be leaving."

Mac reached in his pocket and pulled out a card. He turned it over and wrote his home phone number and cell phone number on the card. He handed it to her.

"If you remember anything or if something else happens, call me."

"Okay. Thanks, Sher…Mac."

She walked him to the door then closed it behind him. He heard the deadbolt set and the chain slide across the metal plate. He walked around the house and noticed in several spots that there were areas of trampled grass. They were located in key spots to see inside if her drapes or blinds were open. He didn't find any other evidence that someone had been there, though. No cigarette butts or candy wrappers.

She knew more than she was telling him. He knew this because she was scared. He had never seen her that shaken before. She was normally a little timid, which was why he and Mason had agreed that, despite their attraction to her, they would leave her alone. But for her to be scared enough to call the department knowing he would be the one to come out, she had to be a lot more scared than she had let on.

She had been avoiding him ever since that night after the Fourth of July picnic nearly five years ago. He had thought that because she seemed friendly, that maybe she would be okay with him and Mason courting her. Unfortunately, she wasn't prepared for both of them at one time, and it had backfired on them. Ever since then they had both kept their distance. Now he was afraid that he couldn't do that anymore. If someone was after her, they would have to go through him to get to her.

Chapter Two

Beth closed the door and slid both the deadbolt and the chain slide closed before all but collapsing against the door. When she lifted up that towel and saw what was in the basket on her front porch, she had stood there looking at her phone for twenty minutes before she got up the nerve to call the sheriff's department. She knew who would end up coming out. She had been right.

Beth hadn't been able to get past that night nearly five years ago when both he and his brother, Mason, had kissed her during the fireworks. She had been so naïve not to have guessed what they were hinting at with their teasing. She knew how things were in Riverbend, Texas. She just hadn't put two and two together with Mac and Mason Tidwell. She had only been twenty-one at the time and was enjoying the bad boys of Riverbend's attention. When they had both kissed her and pressed her to see them, she had nearly passed out in fright. Never in a million years had she thought they were serious, and never would she have thought both of them wanted her at one time.

Now she knew what had scared her so badly back then. It hadn't been them or the idea of a ménage at all. It had been her arousal at their naughty words in her ears. Beth had been appalled that she wanted all of those things and more. She had been turned on, and it frightened her. That is what she had been running from all these years, because God help her, she still wanted all of it, and she wanted it from the Tidwell men.

Mac, with his bald head and tribal tattoo on his bicep, was the bad boy of the two sexy men. His dark eyes could pierce your heart from across the room. He stood a little over six feet five inches and was solid muscle. His square jaw and oval face gave him an air of confidence that most men worked at achieving. He had come by it naturally.

Mason, his younger brother by six minutes, was roughly the same height, but not as muscular as Mac. He had the same dark eyes, but he had a head full of jet black hair that he kept pulled back from his face off his shoulders. Mason was the more refined of the two, but was just as dominant as Mac.

Ever since she had returned from Dallas to live, she had been more than aware of the Tidwell men everywhere she went. It was as if a string attached her to them, so that if they were nearby, she felt them and noticed them. She had purposefully steered clear of Mac and Mason because she believed the attraction on their side was over. Now she wasn't so sure.

And now she had a stalker. She knew that was what he was, because she knew what those items were and what the note meant. He was referring to her last erotic romance novel that had come out a little over two weeks ago. Right after that, she'd had the Peeping Tom, and now this. The feather, the handcuffs, and the candle were all from the book entitled *Everything She Wanted.*

She hadn't told Mac about it because no one in Riverbend knew that she wrote erotic romance. They all thought she did freelance editing for a living, and she did or she had until the book sales had gotten so good. Now she had to work hard to keep up with her writing. Since she didn't write under her own name, someone had found out who she was, and that scared her even more. Someone knew her secrets. She wondered with a sick feeling in her gut if they knew all her little secrets.

After her ill-fated date with Mac and Mason, Beth had called herself a prude and attempted to break out of her comfort zone. She moved to Dallas and started attending classes on Dominance and Submission or the D/s lifestyle. She'd enjoyed it so much she decided to let one of the Doms in the class work with her. One night he took her to a club in Dallas. She'd slowly gotten into the scene only to find out that the Dom she had picked was a little more into it than she was and didn't like being told no.

When the scene went bad and she had to use the club's safe word, she knew she couldn't trust anyone else, so she stopped going to the classes and the club. Now she didn't date at all, because she wasn't satisfied with straight sex anymore. What was the use? She could have an orgasm on her own without the hassle of male egos and emotionless sex.

She moved back to Riverbend and started writing. She used the pen to write out her fantasies. Only now, someone knew they were hers, and it scared the fuck out of her.

Beth knew she couldn't go back to writing now, so she shut down her computer after saving everything to two different drives. She could use a cup of coffee but didn't want to sit in the house alone. She decided to drive to the diner. There would always be someone there drinking coffee or eating pie. She checked her watch. It was pushing two now. She would spend an hour there and clear her head. By then, she should feel up to writing again.

Beth grabbed her purse and keys on the way out the door. She stopped and considered a security system as she looked at the locks. She would research it online when she got back. It really didn't sound like such a bad idea to her.

Ten minutes later she was pulling in the parking lot of the Riverbend Diner. Mattie and her husbands owned it. These days, she had a college kid helping during the evenings and on weekends. The cute girl waved at her and brought over the coffee pot with a mug.

"Hey, Beth. How are you doing?"

"Doing fine, Kelly. How's school going?"

She wrinkled her nose. "It's okay. I just wish I could talk the professor in my English Lit class out of some of the boring books we have to read."

Beth laughed. Kelly enjoyed reading the racier books like hers. Though she had never asked who her favorite authors where, Beth knew she read erotic romance. Kelly had shown her one of her books that she was reading behind the counter one day.

"Don't knock the classics, Kelly."

"So, just coffee or maybe some pie today?"

"I think I'll stick with coffee for now. I'll let you know if I hear a piece of Mattie's pie calling me."

"Got you. I'll be in the back unless someone comes in. Just holler."

Beth settled into the booth with her Kindle and the coffee and began reading. Kelly came by once and refreshed her coffee for her. When she was finished with this cup, she would go back home. Right now, she was in the middle of an especially raunchy sex scene in the book she was reading and didn't notice when someone sat down across from her until he cleared his throat.

Her eyes jerked up from the book and she nearly yelped. Mason sat across from her with a serious expression on his face.

"Um, hey, Mason." She had seen him around a little more than she had seen Mac, but they rarely spoke. What was he doing sitting at her booth?

"Mac said you needed to get a security system. I want you to use these guys. I trust them, and they're reasonably priced."

He laid the card on the table in front of her. She picked it up and looked at the name on it. *Riker Security*. There were two numbers on the card. She turned it over, but it was blank on the back.

"Just tell them I sent you. They'll treat you well and do an excellent job."

"I'm considering getting a system. I was going to do some research on it when I got back home."

"It's already done for you. Use them, Beth. They're the best."

Mason stared at her intensely then nodded and stood up.

"I'll let you finish up your coffee before it gets cold. I just wanted to be sure you called them."

"I'll call them when I get home." She didn't know why she found herself agreeing to call them, but she figured it wouldn't hurt anything to get an estimate.

He smiled, and her heart skipped a beat. Both of the Tidwell men got her juices flowing in no time. She squeezed her legs together and hoped she didn't leave a puddle of goo when she stood up.

When he left, she sipped her now-cool coffee and put away her book. Nothing written could compare with her imagination using Mason and Mac as her inspiration. She pulled out a tip and left it on the table then met Kelly at the register to pay for her coffee.

I saw Mason Tidwell talking to you. Did he ask you out?"

"No. We're old friends. He saw me sitting here and just stopped in to say hi. I don't see him very often."

"Hmm, he stood there and stared at you for quite a while before he came inside."

"He did?" Beth felt her face grow warm.

"Yep, he did. Seems like maybe he likes you a little more than he's letting on. He'll be asking you out before long. You just watch."

She made some comment and left before she said something to embarrass herself. If he really liked her and Mac still liked her, maybe she could...

No, don't go there. It was a long time ago. They've moved on and aren't interested in you anymore. Live with it.

Still, if they were interested, would she play with them now? Did she trust them enough to submit to them? Yeah, she did. Deep down inside she had always known she could trust them. She had screwed up her chance. It was best to face it and keep on going like she had been. She had a satisfactory life. So what if it lacked excitement.

At the thought of excitement, she remembered her stalker, and her stomach sank. She could live with going back to no excitement right about now. This kind of excitement she could do without.

When she returned home, Beth walked around the house to be sure there were no little surprises before unlocking her door and going inside. She locked everything back and fingered the card Mason had given her. She took her cell phone into the office with her and sat down. After a few minutes of procrastination, Beth dialed the number on the card. Someone answered on the third ring.

"Ricker Security."

"Um, yes, Mason Tidwell gave me your card and said you were the best. I need a security system.

"Home, office, or both?"

"Home. My office is in my home."

He got her name, phone number, and address and promised to arrive at nine the next morning to give her an estimate. She hung up feeling like she had made a serious investment in her security and wondered if it was because he sounded so professional, or if she was feeling that scared.

She settled down and got back to writing. After rereading her last chapter, she took off with her book. She didn't stop until she yawned. She looked at her phone and realized it was nearly midnight. She had been writing for almost seven straight hours, stopping only for bathroom breaks. She stretched and yawned again. After saving her usual compulsive two and three times, she headed for the bathroom for a quick shower.

When she got out of the shower, her cell phone was ringing. She frowned, who could it be? She reached for the phone and looked at the caller ID. It was unlisted. She started to not answer it, but then worried that it could be important. Sometimes an editor would call her this late. Still she hesitated. Finally she shrugged and answered it.

"Hello?"

"I'll give you everything."

"Who is this?"

"Did you like my offerings?"

"What do you want?"

"You, Beth. Always you."

He hung up. The voice had been mechanical, so she didn't recognize who it was. What should she do? She thought about calling the sheriff's department, but didn't want to talk to one of the deputies about this. Her breathing had turned to near pants now. She pulled on her sleep shirt and a robe. Then she retrieved Mac's card that he had given her. There were two phone numbers on it besides the sheriff's office number. Should she call? Looking at the phone and remembering the eerie voice, she swallowed and dialed one of the numbers. It rang twice and Mac's voice, a little distant, answered.

"Tidwell."

"Mac? It's Beth."

"What's wrong, Beth?" His voice instantly cleared up.

"I probably should have waited 'til in the morning. I–I'm sorry."

"Don't you fucking hang up the phone!"

"I got a phone call from whoever left the basket."

"What did he say?"

Beth told him and then listened to silence on the other end of the phone.

"I'll be there in a few minutes. Don't open the door to anyone but me, Beth. Not anyone else."

"You don't have to come over. I'm fine. I just needed to tell someone."

"I'm on my way."

Beth heard the click of the phone letting her know he'd disconnected. She swallowed and thought about putting on regular clothes, but he might get there before she had time to get completely dressed. She wasn't far from where he lived. Sure enough, not five minutes later, she heard the telltale sound of tires on gravel as he pulled up behind her Nissan.

"Bethany, open the door." Mac's loud voice sounded strained.

"She looked out the window and found that both Mac and Mason where standing there in jeans and T-shirts on her front porch. She unlocked the door and opened it for them.

"Has he called back?" Mac asked.

"No. I don't think he will. He said what he wanted to say."

"Pack a bag, Bethy." Mason took her arm and led her toward the back of the house where the bedrooms were. He stopped in the hall and looked from one closed door to the other.

"Why do I need to pack a bag?"

"Because until you have a decent alarm system, you're staying with us," he said.

"Let me have your phone, Beth." Mac held out his hand.

Beth looked from one of them to the other and handed her phone over to Mac. Then she led the way into her bedroom to pack a bag. There was no way she could argue with them in the mood they were in. She grabbed her overnight case and stuffed a change of clothes and her toiletry items in it. Then she walked into her office and grabbed her laptop bag and her jump drives. She hurried out of the office and closed the door behind her. She really didn't want either man in there. It was her refuge.

"Did you recognize his voice? Did it even sound familiar to you?" Mac asked.

"It was a mechanical voice. I didn't recognize anything about it."

"Okay, let's go," Mason said.

"Wait, I'm meeting the security guy here in the morning at nine. I need to be sure and be here."

"We'll meet him," Mason said.

Mac took her overnight bag and laptop case while Mason led her to the porch. When she started down the porch, he picked her up and carried her to the truck, scooting her across the front seat to the middle.

"I could have walked."

"The rocks would have hurt your feet through those thin-soled house slippers."

Beth really couldn't say anything to that because he was right. Mason was always right. That was why he was such a good lawyer. His talents were wasted in a little town like Riverbend, but he often worked in Dallas when the occasion arose. She had always wondered why he stuck around, but now that she was older, she knew it was because of the lifestyle. They wanted to live somewhere where how they lived their life didn't matter as long as no one got hurt. In Riverbend, you could have two or three husbands and no one looked at you twice. You could live a D/s relationship out in the open, and it wasn't frowned upon.

Mac finished stowing her bags in the back seat and climbed into the truck. He started the engine and backed out, heading for their home about three or four minutes away.

When they pulled into the drive of the pretty, two-story brick house, she felt a sense of claustrophobia descending on her. Everything seemed to be closing in on her once again. She fought it this time. She wasn't a naïve kid anymore. She knew the lay of the land.

Mason helped her out onto the concrete drive. She followed him in with Mac bringing up the rear, carrying her things. Mason unlocked the door and reset the alarm before they walked inside.

"Did your friends do your security system?" she asked.

"Yeah, they did. We'll get them started on your place right away."

Mason led the way to the stairs and up toward the second floor. He looked over at Mac. Mac nodded, and they led her down a long hall to a closed door. Mason opened it, and inside was a very large bedroom. It held a ménage-size bed with a dresser and two chests. There was an armoire on one wall and three doors on the opposite wall.

"This must be the master suite. Don't you have a smaller room I can bunk in? Or, I can sleep on the couch downstairs. I don't want to mess up this room."

"It's the only room available right now," Mac said. "No, to the couch."

"Okay." She sighed.

Mac set her things on a chair in the room. Then he turned around to walk out. He stopped and spoke from the doorway.

"You did good to call me, Beth. You can always count on either me or Mason to help you if you need us." Then he and Mason walked out and closed the door behind him.

Beth swallowed around the knot in her throat and walked over to the bed. It was massive. There were hidden hooks in the headboard if you really looked. She wasn't a bit surprised. They would want those in any relationship they had. She shivered at the thought of all their attention on her. Sleeping in that bed would be next to impossible. She wouldn't be able to sleep for thinking about what they might do to her in it.

She toyed with her robe buttons for several sad seconds. Then she let out a quick breath and removed it to climb under the covers of the big bed. The minute she settled into the comfortable mattress, she closed her eyes and fell asleep.

Chapter Three

Mac looked at Mason as he searched through Beth's phone. He had tried to redial the last number, but it said that number was no longer in service. No doubt the man had used a prepaid phone that you could buy for twenty bucks anywhere now. It would be at the bottom of a river or in a dumpster somewhere for all he knew.

"She's not telling me everything, Mason. She's hiding something. I just can't figure out what it is, or if it is even part of this mess."

"She's so submissive, Mac."

"I know."

"I can't back away from her this time, Mac. She's in our bed."

"We'll discuss it after we've cleared up whatever the fuck is going on."

"There's nothing to discuss as far as I'm concerned."

Mac ran a hand over his bald head. It was clear Mason had made up his mind, and nothing was going to change it now. Everything would depend on Beth and how she handled their aggressiveness. He wouldn't push her into anything she wasn't ready for. Mac would fight his twin over it if need be. She deserved a normal life if she could have it without all the crap that went along with their lifestyle. If she took to it, though, neither one of them had the strength in them to let her go.

"She makes a lot of phone calls to Dallas and New York." Mac continued to scroll through her phone numbers.

"She's an editor. She probably talks to agents or publishers a lot."

"Well other than those numbers, she has the pizza place, the diner, and the bank. That's it. No friends that I can find."

"I see her out and about town fairly regular, so she isn't staying cooped up alone all the time. She just doesn't make a lot of phone calls outside of work."

"When have you ever seen a woman that doesn't have a phone glued to her ear?" Mac commented.

"True, but she isn't a typical woman, Mac. You know that."

"Have you talked to Lee about setting up her security?"

"Yeah, he knows we want the best and we'll supplement the cost."

"She isn't going to stay here indefinitely, but the longer it takes him to put it in, the safer she'll be. Once she goes back to that house, she's at risk again."

"I'll make sure he knows to drag it out some for us. I don't want her to ever go back to that house."

"She will, though. We can't pursue her while this is going on. Neither one of us can afford to have our balance off, and once she's in our bed, it'll be off."

"I think she's safer once she's in our bed. She'll always be there after that so no one can get to her." Mason ran a hand over his face. "I'm going to go lie down for a couple of hours before we have to be at her house to meet Lee."

"Yeah, I need to do the same thing. I'll talk to you in the morning." Mac watched his brother head to the living room where the stairs were located.

He sat at the kitchen table a little while longer thinking about Beth's lack of obvious friends. She went to Dallas several times a year as well as New York, but other than that she didn't get out much. She'd moved to Dallas that same year of the disastrous Fourth of July weekend then moved back that next year. She had told someone that she just wasn't cut out for big-city living. He'd been relieved to see her back. He had missed seeing her, missed thinking that maybe one day they might still have a chance at happiness.

He stood up and stretched. Then he carried her phone up to his bedroom, where he sat it on the bedside table. After stripping down to his boxers, he stretched out on top of the covers to sleep. Only sleep wasn't in the cards for him tonight. All he could do was think about Beth and how much he wanted her.

His cock was rock hard and throbbing. It had been since he had seen her that morning. There was no way he was going to get to sleep like he was. He shoved his boxers down his thighs and grasped his dick at the base and squeezed as he pulled up. Then he did it again, and a drop of pre-cum pearled at the slit on top of the crown. He rubbed it around the mushroom head for lubrication and began to tug on it over and over as he imagined Beth's lips stretched wide around his cock. She would stare up at him as she sucked on his dick. He could almost feel the suction of her mouth as she went down on him.

Mac ran his hand up and down the long stalk of his cock. He reached between his legs and cupped his balls then massaged them in their sac. He'd love for her to take his balls in her mouth and roll them with her tongue. More pre-cum seeped from the slit at the top of his dick. He captured it and rolled it up and down his cock with his hand as he tugged harder and harder.

Beth would lick up and down the stalk before taking just the head of him into her mouth to suck. She would lick over the slit in the crown to taste the cum leaking there. Then she would suck him down to the back of her throat.

He continued to pull on his balls as he tugged at his cock. He could feel the fire at the base of his spine begin to grow. His balls tightened as he got closer to his climax. He began to stroke his cock faster as he thought about Beth's mouth wrapped around him. He wanted her to swallow him all the way down her throat. She could do it. He knew she could.

She would relax her throat and breathe through her nose while he fed his aching cock deeper into her mouth until his cockhead touched the back of her throat and she swallowed around him. Just the thought of all that suction did it for him. His balls erupted, shooting long ribbons of cum from his cock onto his belly. He continued stroking until he had squeezed every last drop of cum from his shaft.

Mac lay there for several seconds until he could breathe again then got up and grabbed a cloth to clean up. He sat back on the bed, exhausted. He hoped he would rest some now. He needed to be at the top of his game while there was any danger to Beth.

He slowly lay back down and drifted off into an uneasy sleep.

* * * *

Beth woke to someone shaking her. She screamed when she opened her eyes and saw Mason and Mac standing there. They were both dressed, Mac in his uniform and Mason in jeans and a T-shirt. Where was she? Then it all came back, and she knew she had been dreaming.

"Are you okay?" Mason asked.

She nodded and pulled the covers back up to cover her exposed skin. She wondered how much of her body they had seen. She was only wearing a large T-shirt and panties, and the covers had been around her knees.

"You were screaming, Beth. Do you want to talk about it?" Mac asked with a strained expression on his face.

"I don't remember what I was dreaming about."

Mason started to say something, but Mac shook his head. He frowned but didn't continue. She wondered what that was all about.

"Um, I better get dressed. What time is it?"

"It's a little after seven. You have time for a shower and some breakfast before we meet Lee."

They looked at her with knowing expressions, and she wondered what she had been screaming about.

They turned and walked out of the bedroom, closing the door behind them. Beth quickly crawled out of the bed and remade it before scrambling into the bathroom for a shower. It was a huge room with a large, walk-in shower made of stone and ceramic tile. The whirlpool tub was large enough for three people as well. She didn't let herself imagine what all had gone on in that bedroom and bathroom. She didn't want to know.

Instead she tried to remember what she had been dreaming about. Usually she dreamed about that last time she had been at The Dungeon in Dallas. If she had been dreaming about that, there was no telling what she had been saying. *Not good, Beth. They don't need to know about that period of your life.*

She quickly dressed in a clean pair of jeans and a green blouse. She slipped on her shoes and repacked everything back in her bag. She would need to take it back with her to the house for a new set of clothes if she were going to stay more than one night.

When she emerged from the bedroom, she tried to remember how to get back to the kitchen. She followed the long hall down to the stairs then around the living room to the kitchen. She smiled when she found it.

"There you are. How are you feeling now?" Mason asked.

"I'm fine. You have a really nice bathroom."

"Thanks," they both said.

She accepted the coffee Mac gave her, taking a sip and sighing in pleasure. They must have ground their own beans. It tasted really fresh.

"What would you like for breakfast?" Mac asked.

"I usually just have cereal. Do you have any?"

"Afraid not. I'll scramble you an egg and toast. How about that?" Mac asked.

"That's fine. You really don't have to go to so much trouble. I can just drink coffee and get an early lunch later."

"That's not good for you." Mason shook his head. "You need to eat regular meals."

Beth frowned at him. She didn't need a lecture. Never mind that he was right and she rarely ate on a schedule with her writing like it was.

"Don't frown at me like that. You know I'm right."

"I'm a grown woman. I can take care of myself."

"Mason."

Beth could tell that the two men were a little at odds concerning her. She hated that, but she didn't belong to them. They had no say in her life. She nearly sighed out loud. As much as she would love for them to have a say in her life, it wasn't happening.

After breakfast, Mac left them to go to the office and work on some paperwork he said he needed to catch up on.

"Does he work seven days a week?" she asked before she thought about it.

"Sometimes. He doesn't have a lot to keep him busy here, so he just spends most of his free time at the office." He finished putting away the dishes. "Let's go get your overnight bag and head on over to your house. You're going to need to pack more clothes. You'll be here until we get that security system installed."

"I can't stick around that long. I have my job to do."

"You can work from here. You have your laptop."

"It's just not the same as being in my own space. Can't I work there during the day and come here to sleep at night?"

Mason frowned at her and shook his head.

Beth gritted her teeth and went to grab her case. This was not going to work out.

They arrived back at her house in plenty of time to meet the security guy, Lee. She emptied her dirty clothes into her laundry room, and when she returned to the bedroom to refill her case, it was to find Mason opening her larger suitcase on the bed.

"Do you have a problem filling this up or should I help you pack?"

Beth's mouth worked like a fish before she finally shut it and started packing. She ended up with enough clothes for five days. She wasn't happy in the least. Mason had stood over her the entire time. Then when she had finished, he closed it and took it out to his truck. On his way back, a van pulled up in the drive behind him. He went and shook the man's hand and walked him up to the house. Beth walked out on the porch to meet who she assumed would be the security man.

"Beth, this is Lee Riker. He's going to be putting in your security system."

"I need an estimate first," she said in her sweetest voice.

"Of course, I'll have that in just a few minutes. Do you mind if I look around?"

"No, go right ahead."

"Is there a basement or cellar on the property?"

"No."

"What about an attic large enough for someone to get up inside?"

"Yes, the only entrance to it is in the laundry room in the ceiling."

"Fine. I'll be looking around. It will probably take me about thirty minutes."

"Okay, thanks." She watched him walk inside with a sketch pad and a tape measure.

"Let's sit outside on the porch while he's walking through the house," Mason suggested.

Beth nodded and chose the rocking chair, leaving the swing for him. She didn't want to sit with him too close. She wasn't sure she could control her hands. They itched to run up and down his arms or better yet, over his chest.

"Do you remember any more about your dream this morning?"

The question caught her off guard.

"Not really."

"What do you remember?"

"Just that someone was after me and I knew I couldn't get away."

"Do you have that dream often?"

"No, I used to years ago, but I haven't in a long time. I'm sure this business with having a stalker is what triggered it again."

"You're probably right. You will be safe with us, though, Beth. Do you believe me?"

"Yes. I believe that if anyone could keep me safe it would be you and Mac."

He nodded. A few minutes later, Lee walked out with a grim look on his face.

"What?" Beth asked.

"Come with me. I need to show you some things."

Beth didn't have a good feeling about this. She didn't pull away when Mason held her hand and walked through the house with her following Lee.

He took her to her office. She cringed. Surely he didn't snoop through her things. He pointed to her desk to a screw on the side. He wrote on a piece of paper. *That is a bug.* Mason immediately put a hand over her mouth to assure that she didn't say anything. When he let go, she nodded. Heat rose to her cheeks to realize that someone had been listening to her talk through her scenes. Then he curled his finger for them to follow him. He closed that door and took them into her bedroom. He had them stand back by her dresser. Then he lifted the top off the smoke detector.

"This is a camera. It doesn't have sound with it so you can talk in here. I didn't find any bugs in here."

"That camera was aimed at my bed, wasn't it?"

"Yes, ma'am. I'm afraid that it was."

Mason squeezed her hand in his.

"How did they get in the house?"

"A really good thief can break in to any of these locks. They're good for petty thieves, but won't stop an experienced one. Personally, I think the stalker has a key to your house. There's no sign of tampering with any of the locks. He either has a master key or an actual key. He could have gotten one by making a copy of one of yours when you left it somewhere handy for him to make an imprint with wax or modeling clay."

"What do I do now?"

"I figured Mac will want to see about all of this before we start work on your security system."

"He will. Can we call you when he finishes?" Mason asked.

"That's fine. I'll be waiting on your call."

"Thanks Lee. I owe you on this one."

"It was my pleasure. I hate seeing a pretty woman terrorized in her own home." He winked at her and headed for his van.

"I don't believe it. Someone has been watching me sleep at night. They've been listening to me when I'm working or on the phone in my office." Beth felt a bubble lodge in her throat making her want to scream.

"Easy, baby. We need to go talk to Mac about this. Is there anything else you need out of the house before we leave. You likely won't be allowed in the house again for several days after this."

"Oh, God. I need to get some notes and things from my office so I can work."

"Let's go do that and then we're going to go to talk to Mac."

Beth felt like her entire life was crumbling around her. Her perfect sanctuary had been a farce all this time. She knew now that no matter what, everything was going to come out now. Mac would find out everything if he snooped through her things in the office, and he would since there had been a bug in her office.

She grabbed a plastic file box and grabbed all her notes on the book she was working on and stuffed it in the box. Then she looked around and noticed all the little things that would tip Mac off that she wasn't who she pretended to be anymore. She would have to tell him.

She started to walk out of the office with the box, but Mason took it from her. He walked beside her back to the front of the house and out onto the porch. She locked the door and walked back out to his truck. Once inside, she looked out the side window, not wanting to talk.

"It's going to be okay, Beth."

"No it's not. Nothing will ever be the same again. My world just got knocked out from under me, Mason. Everything I've worked so hard to build is gone. All my privacy, my sanctuary, it's all gone."

"I'm sorry, baby. I wish I could do something to make it all go away." He patted her thigh then cranked the truck and backed out of the drive.

Chapter Four

When they drove up to the sheriff's office, Mason got out of the truck and walked around to help her out. She hadn't even unbuckled her seatbelt. She couldn't think. He swung her down and led her up the steps with a hand to the small of her back. It was comforting in a way. Right now, she felt mostly numb inside.

Mac met them just inside the door.

"What's wrong?"

"We need to talk in your office," Mason said.

Mac led them back to his office where he drew the blinds and locked the door.

"What happened?"

Mason filled him in on what Lee had found. Mac watched her face the entire time he was talking. His face showed nothing, his expression, utterly blank. Then he stood up and paced over to the door and back.

"Okay, I'm going to take a team and go through your house, Beth. This is more than a simple stalker case. He's a planner and is highly intelligent. That's a dangerous combination. Is there something you need to tell me before we go any further?"

Mason's eyebrows drew together. He looked as if he would say something, but he kept quiet.

"I'm an erotic romance writer. I write under the pen name of Harley James. The things in that basket were from m–my last book called, *Everything She Wanted*"

"What are we going to find in your house, Beth?"

"My books, some props and toys. My contracts and various other paperwork about my writing." She didn't look at him. She couldn't look at him or Mason.

"Anything else, baby?" Mason asked her.

"No. Isn't that enough?"

"No movies or pictures?"

"No!" She jerked her head up to look at Mac now.

"I had to be sure. I wasn't going to send my guys in there if they were going to find something they had no business seeing. Some toys and erotic books are no big deal, babe."

"It will get out that that I write erotic romance, won't it?"

"Not if I can help it, it won't," Mac told her. "There's no need for any of them to ever say anything. I'll reiterate that when we go through your house."

"Okay." She felt the tears in the back of her eyes, but she fought them. They burned, but she didn't want them to fall. Not until she was alone.

"Is there anything else I need to know about, Beth?"

She looked up then back down. Was there any reason to go through all that? Did he need to know for the stalker?

She swallowed. "Can we talk about it at your house away from here? I really don't think it has anything to do with this. It was a long time ago."

Mac gritted his teeth but nodded. "We'll talk about it tonight."

"Can I have my phone back now? I need to talk to my agent and my publisher to let them know that I'll be out of pocket for a while."

"You can use one of our phones, Beth," Mason offered.

"I don't know all the numbers. I have them written down at the house, but I'm used to just pushing the buttons to dial them."

Mac reached in his pocket and pulled out the phone. He handed it to her.

"If he contacts you by that phone, you give it to either me or Mason. Do you understand?"

"I will."

"Mason, take her home and keep her there. I'll be home as soon as we finish with her house. Call me if she gets a phone call."

"I will." He reached for Beth's hand and helped her out of the chair. "Let's go, baby. I suspect you could use a nap."

Beth moved in a fog. She didn't even remember riding back to their house or getting in the truck. The next thing she knew, they were walking inside their home and Mason was setting the security. She drew in a deep breath and looked around the kitchen.

"Mason?"

"Yeah, baby?"

"I need a drink. Do you have anything here?"

"We've got beer."

"That will do. I have to call my agent and my publisher. I can't call my publisher until tomorrow, but I can call my agent at home."

Mason pulled a beer out of the fridge and opened it before handing it to her. She accepted it and thanked him. Then she walked into the living room and sat on the couch after kicking off her shoes. She curled up and punched in Ann's number.

"Hello?"

"Hey, Ann, it's Bethany."

"Hey, woman. Is something wrong? You don't sound like yourself, and you're calling me on a Sunday morning."

"Someone has found out my real name. I'm being stalked and have to go under the radar for a while. I wanted to let you know I'll be out of pocket."

"Are you okay? Do you need a bodyguard? I have the names of some reputable companies."

"Thanks, Ann, but I've got that part covered. I just wanted to let you know I might not be able to call or answer my phone for a few days."

"What about your book? Do I need to talk to the publisher for you about an extension?"

"I really don't think so. I'm ahead of schedule on it right now. I was going to call them tomorrow anyway and let them know what was going on."

"You let me deal with them. I'll tell them, and you can get under cover that much quicker."

"If something happens and I need time on the book, I'll let you know. Thanks for dealing with the publisher for me."

"That's part of my job, honey. You stay safe, and let me know as soon as you can that you're safe."

"I will, bye."

"That was good. You didn't give her any information. That was smart." Mason walked over and sat next to her on the couch. "Can I get you anything else?"

"No, I think I'm going to take a nap. I didn't get much sleep last night."

"Neither did I. I think I'll take one with you."

It didn't even occur to Beth that he meant to sleep with her in the same bed until he followed her into the bedroom. She looked over at him. He just smiled and pulled off his shoes. Beth sighed and pulled off her shoes and climbed up on the big bed and curled up on the edge. The next thing she knew, Mason had pulled her back into his arms.

"Sleep, baby. I'll watch over you."

Despite thinking that she could never go to sleep with him next to her, she did.

* * * *

Mac didn't make it home until nearly eight that night. He pulled into the drive and cut off the truck but didn't get out immediately. He needed to calm down before he walked inside. He was furious that someone had bugged and videoed Beth's home. Not only was she being terrorized, but her privacy had been invaded.

He was also very surprised to find that their timid little Beth wrote some of the hottest books he'd ever read, everything from BDSM to ménage. He had a hard time wrapping his head around it. All this time they had been worried about scaring her and stayed away from her, and she was teaching others about it.

He shook his head and finally climbed out of the truck carrying a few things from her house in a bag. He unlocked the door then reactivated the security. Mason met him in the kitchen.

"Hey, everything finished?"

"Yeah. We found one more camera in her bathroom. It was in the vanity mirror. Don't tell her. There's no need for her to know. It will just upset her."

"I agree. We took a nap for a couple of hours when we got home. She's been writing ever since. I think she uses it to hide away."

"Is she okay for a few minutes?" Mac asked.

"Yea, I just checked on her. What?"

"Follow me."

He carried the bag to the back of the house where they had a playroom in what used to be the carport. It was soundproofed and under a keypad lock. He decoded it, and they walked in then closed and locked the door back. Mac opened the bag and pulled out several of her books.

"She wrote these?" Mason asked.

"Yep. They're very good, too. Very accurate. She knows her BDSM, Mason."

"Do you think she's experimented with it?"

"I would think she would have had to in order to get it down as well as she has."

"So we have a chance with her."

"I honestly don't know, Mason. Why isn't she living the lifestyle if she likes it? There has to be a reason behind it."

"Do you think what she plans to tell us tonight has anything to do with it?"

"Yeah, I do. I have a feeling we're not going to like what she has to tell us."

"Fuck!"

"Get it out of your system now, because if we react wrong, it could screw up our chances with her, Mason."

"What else do you have in that bag?"

"Some of her toys. I was suitably surprised to find a butt plug, a wand, and a silver bullet."

Mason's eyes lit up. "We can have fun with those."

"Maybe later. First we have to get through whatever she's going to tell us. Then we have to catch this fucking asshole stalking her. Then we can play."

Mac left everything in the playroom except the book that had caused the problems. They locked up behind them and walked back into the living room. Mac dropped the book on the coffee table then went in search of Beth. It was time to talk.

He knocked on the door to the master suite and walked in. He didn't want to barge in and startle her. He figured she was deep into her writing. Instead, he found her sitting on the floor by the bed with her eyes closed. He walked over and knelt beside her.

"Beth?"

Her eyes opened, and he could tell that she'd been crying at some point in the day. There was still some residual redness around her eyes.

"Beth, how about something to drink?"

"I could use a margarita if you want to know the truth about it."

"Drinking isn't the answer, babe."

"I know, but it sure helps." She swallowed and leaned forward to get up.

Mac stood up and helped her to her feet.

"Mason thought you were up here writing."

"I have been. I just stopped and needed to relax."

"Why on the floor by the bed?"

"Because I hoped if there was a camera up there it wouldn't see me." Tears fell once again, but she quickly dried them and drew in a deep breath. "I suppose you want to talk now."

"Yeah, we need to get everything out in the open, Beth."

"Okay." She walked toward the door. He opened if for her and led her downstairs to the living room where Mason had poured a glass of wine for her.

"I thought all you had was beer," she accused.

"No, I said we had beer. I just didn't tell you we had wine, too. I figured you might need it later." Mason grinned at her.

She scowled right back at him but took the glass from him and sipped from it.

"Mmm, good."

"Glad you approve. Have a seat, Beth. What did you not want to talk about at the office?"

"Do you remember when we um, had the little misunderstanding at the Fourth of July picnic?"

"Misunderstanding, that's one way of putting it," Mason said.

"Yeah, well. I felt like such a prude. I was more afraid of myself than I was of you or Mac. All of those things you talked about turned me on and made me want them. It scared me, so I ran. I kept on running until I moved to Dallas later that year. I was so ashamed of myself. I found out about some classes on BDSM and started taking the them. Then I went to some lifestyle classes and that led to the clubs.

"You fucking went to BDSM clubs?" Mac yelled.

"Easy, Mac." Mason had stood when Mac jumped up.

Mac slowly sat back down with a scowl on his face.

"Do you have any idea how dangerous that was, Beth?"

"Yes, but I was with a group. We all watched out for each other, and we were under two Masters who led the studies. They had excellent reputations."

"Who were they?" Mac demanded.

"I'm not telling you yet. When I finish, if you want to know, I'll tell you."

"Fair enough," he groused.

"Anyway, we all started looking for our own Doms and subs. One of the guys who had gone through the entire program with us asked to by my Dom. I talked it over with the Masters, and they thought it would be an excellent match. We seemed to have, um, complementary needs."

"What sort of needs do you have, Beth?" Mason asked.

"Mason, let her finish, and then we'll find out exactly what our little Beth needs."

Beth shivered.

"Go on, Beth," Mac said.

"Well, things were going well. I eventually moved in with him. He knew I didn't want the lifestyle twenty-four-seven, but that I wanted it more often than the occasional scene. Then one night something happened, and he snapped. We were at The Dungeon and had set up a scene typical for us."

"Describe the scene, Beth."

Mac walked over to the bar and poured more wine in her glass. He had a feeling she was going to need it. Hell he probably needed it.

"Saint Andrew's Cross. I was buckled to it, nude. He had already inserted the butt plug and used the flogger on me. He was going to use the single tail next. We always ended with ten licks from it. I was sweating, and the cuffs felt tighter than usual. I knew it was almost the end anyway, so I didn't use my safe word. He warmed me up with four stings that hurt, but weren't that bad. Then he began to lay into me. I lost count after eight, they hurt so badly. I gave up and called out my safe word, but he didn't stop. I screamed it out over and over but he still didn't stop."

"Jesus," Mason said. "Why didn't someone stop him?"

"No one knew my safe word that was there that night. None of our usual group had come to The Dungeon with us." She took another sip of the wine and another one. "Finally, I remembered the club safe word and screamed *red* out over and over again. They tell me that someone had to grab him and pull the whip out of his hands, because he wasn't listening. He'd snapped and lost it. No one knew what caused it or why it happened."

"How bad were you, Beth?" Mac finally asked.

Beth sighed and sipped her wine. Then she stood up and pulled her T-shirt over her head and turned her back to them.

"Fucking son of a bitch!" Mac couldn't believe the thin scars on her back. There were easily six that he could see. If he looked closely, he saw maybe four or five more.

"They said when they got me down, I was covered in blood, and my wrists and ankles were bloodied as well from how tight the cuffs had been on them. They had a doctor on call specifically for accidental injuries, and he treated me in his home for a week."

"Aw fuck, baby." Mason walked around in front of her and pulled her into his arms.

"They contacted our Masters who immediately came down to figure out what had gone wrong. They tell me that they never did determine what happened to my Dom. He ended up in a mental institution. He had totally lost touch with reality."

She let Mason hug her, but she didn't hug him back. Mac decided she had stepped outside of herself to tell the story. It was probably less traumatic that way.

"Anyway, once I was well again, I moved back to Riverbend. I had been editing for nearly a year by then anyway and had gotten fed up with some of the BDSM books I edited being way off base. So, I started writing my own and sold one. Then I sold another and another. They helped me work through the experience."

"Who was the Dom that did this to you, Beth?"

"Do you really need to know, Mac? He's somewhere that he can't hurt anyone else."

"I want to know his name."

"Larry Jordan."

"Are you sure that he is still in the mental institution?" Mason asked.

"They were supposed to let me know if he ever got out. No one has contacted me."

"I think I'll do some digging on him tomorrow," Mac said. "Let's get you ready for bed, babe. I think you're a bit tipsy."

"Ya think?" She smiled and picked up her T-shirt after draining the last of her wine.

Mac and Mason walked her upstairs, making sure she didn't fall then walked her down the hall to the bedroom. Mac pulled back the bed sheets and Mason helped him remove her shoes and jeans.

"I have to take my bra off. I don't like to sleep in it." She flicked the front closure on it and let it fall off. Mason groaned at the sight of her breasts unfettered.

"Let's get her in the bed before we do something reprehensible," Mac said.

He picked her up and laid her gently on the bed. Mason pulled the cover up around her chin, and then kissed her lightly on the lips.

They backed out of the bedroom once they were sure she was indeed asleep. Once they got back downstairs to the living room, Mac had managed to get control of himself once again. He took the empty wine glass and put it in the dishwasher.

"Do you think it could be this Larry fellow?"

"Could be, but I won't know until I find out if he's still an inpatient or not."

"She's afraid to trust, isn't she? That's why she doesn't have friends and she doesn't date. Her friends let her down, and her Dom didn't honor her safe word. How can we ever expect her to trust us after that?" Mason asked.

"I don't know. I can't say that I blame her either. She did everything right, Mason. She found a reputable Master and went to classes and made sure of what she wanted before she ever played. I can't find fault with anything she did."

"I can't give her up, Mac. She's in my blood. If we can't have that sort of relationship with her, then I'm fine with that. I'll live without it."

"Mason. Before you relegate yourself to a lifetime outside the life, let's wait and see what she's willing to do. We can't make any decisions until this lunatic is caught."

"Right now, all that matters is keeping her safe," Mason agreed.

Chapter Five

Mason rolled over, expecting to snuggle up to Beth. Instead, he found an empty pillow. Panic hit him. He rolled out of bed and started to run out of the room to look for her when he heard the water running in the shower. He sighed and opened the bathroom door. Immediately steam swirled out of the room. He stepped inside and closed the door to keep the warmth in the room.

"Mason, Mac?"

"It's me, baby. Mind if I join you?"

"What?"

He walked around the stone wall and stepped into the stinging spray of the multihead shower. Beth yelped and tried to cover herself with her cloth.

"Hey! You can wait until I get out, Mason."

"I don't want to. I want to bathe you. Give me your cloth and turn around."

"Mason?"

"Shh, baby. It's okay. I'm just going to bathe you, that's all." He held out his hand for the cloth.

Beth handed it over and turned around. He soaped up the bath cloth and scrubbed her back. He knew that the scars were years old, but he still found himself wanting to be careful of them as he cleaned her. He scrubbed all down her back and over her ass. Then he turned her around to rinse. When he started bathing her shoulders and her chest, she watched him with uneasy eyes. He hated to see it there, but understood it better now.

"I'm not going to hurt you, baby. I'm just going to bathe you and make you feel good."

He massaged the soap into her breasts with his bare hands. He didn't pinch or pull on her nipples because he didn't want there to be even the hint of pain. Instead, he stroked and licked her nipples, then moved down to her waist and pelvis. He smoothed over her skin with the soapy cloth and moved to clean between her thighs. Then he bathed her legs and feet. One at a time, he lifted each foot and cleaned them before rinsing and placing a kiss on top of them.

She moaned when he kissed her pelvis and worked his way down to her trimmed pussy. He gently spread her legs so that he could get between them. She didn't resist him. It was a good sign. He spread her pussy lips and licked from slit to clit and back down again. Her moan was music to his ears. She tasted like sweet ambrosia to him. He could lap at her pussy all night.

The more he licked, the more honey she produced. Finally, she rested her hands on his head, kneading his scalp with her nails. His cock, already rock hard, began to petrify. It throbbed with need.

Beth's moans began to change to little mews as he circled her clit with his tongue. He rasped over it once, and she went up on her toes with a soft cry. Adding a finger to her hot cunt, Mason slowly pumped it in and out of her. She groaned and thrashed her head from side to side. He continued his oral assault as his finger sought her hot spot deep in her cunt. When he added a second finger, she dug her claws into his head and tugged on his hair. He lapped at her pussy juices as they coated his face.

When he knew she was right there, hot and ready, he latched on to her clit with his lips and sucked as he stroked her sweet spot until she screamed out in climax. He slowly licked her down from her orgasm-induced high until she started to collapse against him. He easily caught her before she fell. Standing up, Mason wrapped his arms around her and kissed her forehead. His throbbing cock was cushioned between them.

He figured he better get her out of the shower and dried off before it registered that he was rock hard against her belly. He shuffled her out of the shower then grabbed a towel and began to gently pat her dry. She finally started to regain her composure and wrapped the towel around herself. Without looking at him, Beth stepped out of the bathroom, crossing to her suitcase where she rummaged through it until she had found what she wanted.

Mason pulled on his jeans and waited for her to dress. When she was finished, they walked downstairs together. She still hadn't said anything, and Mason was beginning to wonder if she would.

"Would you like some coffee?"

"Yes, please." She looked around the kitchen before settling at the bar.

Mason busied himself making the coffee and then looked in the fridge for ingredients for breakfast.

"Why did you do that?"

"Make you come?"

"Yeah, because you didn't."

"It wasn't about me. It was about you. I wanted you to feel good. With everything going on, you're tense and upset. I hoped an orgasm would relax you a little bit."

When she didn't say anything more, he sighed and poured the coffee and handed her a cup. Then he went back to cooking.

"Thanks, Mason."

"It was my pleasure, I assure you," he said with a grin.

Beth rolled her eyes and everything seemed to be okay after that.

Mac walked into the kitchen about the time breakfast was ready. He grunted good morning then poured himself a cup of the brew. He settled on the barstool next to Beth and took a sip. He stared at her speculatively. Mason wondered if he had been awake or if Beth's cry had awakened him.

"How did you sleep, Beth?"

"Pretty good. I just woke up and couldn't go back to sleep."

"Mac, I need to go into the office for a while. I have a case in court later this week and need to prepare for it."

"Beth can go to the station with me. I'll set her up at an empty desk to write."

"Hey, I'm right here. I can't write at a sheriff's office. I need complete quiet, and sometimes I talk to myself while I'm writing. Can't I stay here? You have a good security system."

"I don't want to take a chance."

"Please, Mac. I'll be safe here. I need to write."

Mac and Mason exchanged looks, and Mason shrugged.

"Our security system is top of the line."

"Hell, okay. You can stay here and write as long as you don't go anywhere or open the door to anyone."

"I won't. I'll stay upstairs and write until you guys get back. I promise."

"If your phone rings, don't answer it if you don't recognize the number. Call me instead, and I'll come home in case he calls back."

"Okay, I won't answer the phone unless I know who it is."

"I don't like it."

"I promise I won't open the door or answer the phone if I don't know who it is. All I'm going to do is write."

"I'll be home around lunchtime." He would make sure that he was. He could bring his case files home with him.

"Okay, Beth. You can stay." Mac looked less than happy about it.

Mason didn't blame him. He wasn't too thrilled with it either, but knew that Beth would probably fight over her writing. They didn't need to alienate her with a stalker in the picture.

They finished eating breakfast in silence. Then Beth dealt with the dishes, leaving him free to leave early. He reminded her that he would be back around lunchtime.

"I'll bring something home to eat. Any preferences?"

"No, a sandwich or burger is fine with me."

He nodded at Mac and grabbed his briefcase on the way to the door. Once in the car, he attempted to put Beth out of his mind and concentrate on his case. That proved next to impossible. He figured he would do better with that once he got to the office.

As soon as he opened the door, the secretary was up with a cup of coffee and his messages. There were quite a few. He sighed. That would take some time.

"Don't forget you have a meeting with Ted Madison at three."

"Call and reschedule that one. I have something else going on. Make it for several days off if you can. He just wants to talk mostly. If he needs something major, see if Fields can help him this time."

"Mason? Is something wrong?"

Sandra, the office secretary, was in her fifties and tended to mother him. She meant well, but he didn't need her prodding today.

"Nothing, Sandra. I just have some other business that I have to attend to today. I'm going to be in and out over the next few days. Plus, I have that court case on Thursday."

"Okay. I'll take care of Mr. Madison."

"Thanks, Sandra."

He continued into his office and closed the door. Then he set up his workspace and pulled out his briefs to review. After thirty minutes of reading the same page and not getting anywhere, Mason cursed and moved on to answer his messages.

It took him almost two hours to take care of them. Everyone needed something and expected him to be able to provide it. He ran a hand over his face. He wasn't usually this impatient with his clients. He was worried about Beth. At the same time, he was fighting the hard-on of all hard-ons.

He'd nearly lost it when she'd come earlier in the shower. Seeing her lose some of her careful control as her body turned a pretty shade of pink had nearly made him come just watching her. Waiting for Mac to catch the lunatic stalking her was going to test all of his patience. He wanted to tie her to the bed and watch her come over and over again.

His cock pressed tight against the zipper of his dress pants. Walking to his truck was going to be uncomfortable to say the least. He gathered up everything he thought he would need to finish preparing for his case and repacked his briefcase. Then he called the diner and ordered sandwiches to take back home. He wasn't sure what kind to get for Beth, so he ordered several different kinds.

Driving over to pick them up, Mason thought about what Beth had told them the night before. If he had known what she had been doing in Dallas, he would have gone and gotten her. He and Mac could have shown her anything she wanted to know about. The fact that strangers had taught her didn't sit well with him. He felt as if he had failed her. They should have been able to decipher her reaction and realized she was curious but scared.

Then again, maybe not. It was all in the past now. There was nothing he could do to change it. Seeing those scars on her back had nearly made him go crazy. He never lost it. He was always the one in total control where Mac would blow up. Beth was his Achilles' heel. She always had been.

* * * *

Beth finally settled down enough to write thirty minutes after the men had gone. She set up her computer along with her notes at the dining room table. It wasn't the ideal place, but it would work. After fooling around with everything, trying to get into the mood, she started working.

The words wouldn't flow like they normally did, and she grew frustrated. As she stared at the nearly empty screen, thoughts of her and Mason in the shower that morning poured over her. Her face grew hot and her pussy wept. She could almost feel Mason's tongue lapping at her pussy lips. She pressed her thighs together in an effort to recreate part of that feeling. If her pussy grew any damper, she'd have to get a towel for the chair she was sitting on.

As her breath became ragged, she put her hands on the keyboard and began to type. The words leapt from her fingers and appeared on the computer screen. She went with them without thinking about it. Nothing short of an earthquake would interfere with her when she was in the zone. She compared it to that level of subspace that a bottom could attain during a scene.

Sometime later, she heard a noise in the kitchen and froze. She glanced at her phone and noted that it was already nearly noon. She sighed. It was probably Mason. Sure enough, he walked into the living room so that she could see him. She got up and walked into the other room. Mason must have heard her, because he turned around and smiled.

"I brought lunch."

"Great. I'm starved. Did you finish at the office?"

"In a manner of speaking." He indicated the briefcase and books he had placed on the coffee table.

"Ah, you brought work home. Mason, you could have stayed at the office. I'm fine here. I'm working, so I'm perfectly fine."

"Come on. Let's eat. I'm hungry, too."

Beth followed Mason into the kitchen where he opened the bags and spread out the sandwiches. Then he pulled down plates and handed one to her.

"Take your pick. There are several different kinds. I wasn't sure what you liked."

Beth looked at them and chose a turkey club. He poured chips on a third plate for them to share. They ate in silence for several minutes. Then Mason cleared his throat and caught her attention.

"Where did you set up to write? I should have shown you were the office was so you could set up in there."

"I decided on the dining room table. I hope that's okay."

"That's fine. If you want to move to the office later, I'll help you."

"I'm fine where I am. Besides, you may need the office for work since you brought it home with you."

"There's plenty of room for you as well. We have two desks in there. Mac uses one of them sometimes when he's working from home."

"Thanks, but I'm settled now."

"Any phone calls?"

"No. I don't get many anyway. My agent took care of calling my publisher for me, so I didn't have to do that."

"Did anyone ring the doorbell or knock on the door?"

"No. Nothing happened. I've just been writing."

They finished their lunch, and she helped Mason clean up. Then she returned to the dining room and prepared to write again. She heard Mason in the other room gathering his things to take them to the office across the living room. She could see him from where she sat. Then he moved out of her range of vision toward the office she guessed.

Beth wasn't sure how she was going to concentrate now with him in the house. Her mind kept going back to the shower and the fact that he was just a few yards away. She could imagine walking into the office and closing the door behind her. She would cross the room and walk up to where he would be sitting in the chair behind the desk. Then she would turn him toward her and go to her knees in front of him.

He would look down at her with desire in his eyes and brush his finger across her lips. If she were quick, she might lick his finger before he moved it out of reach, maybe even suck it into her mouth.

He'd shake his head and tell her she was a bad girl. He would have to punish her later. Beth could only imagine what sort of punishment he would choose. She knew it would be something delicious. Something she would thoroughly enjoy.

She would reach up and carefully unfasten his slacks and pull down the zipper to expose his silk boxers. Then she would pull his engorged cock from them and run her hands over it. It would feel like silk-encased steel in her hands. She would lick her lips and look up at him for permission. When he gave it, Beth sighed and ran her tongue from bottom to top and around the crest of the mushroom head. Then she would lick the slit at the top to taste the little pearl of pre-cum as he hissed out a breath.

"Fuck, do that again, baby."

She licked over the slit again. She sucked in just his cockhead, using her teeth to rake lightly at the ridge. When he grabbed her head to dig his fingers into her scalp, she moaned around him and sucked him down. Then she came back up and licked around the stalk, paying close attention to the vein that ran the length of his dick.

She memorized every bump and vein with her tongue and mouth as she took him to the back of her throat over and over again. Finally, she swallowed around him while she had him down her throat. He cursed and dug into her scalp before pulling her off of him.

"I'm going to come if you keep doing that."

"Isn't that the goal?"

"Aw, hell. Suck my cock, baby. Take it all the way down, and make me come."

Beth redoubled her efforts at driving him wild. She wanted him unable to do anything but hold her head and fuck her mouth. When he finally lost control, he controlled her head as he began to thrust inside her mouth in short shallow pumps of his pelvis. Slowly he deepened his strokes until he was bumping the back of her throat with nearly every pump of his cock into her mouth.

Finally, he began to lose his rhythm. She held onto his thighs as he roared out his release and spurted cum down her throat in long ribbons. She swallowed it all and then licked him clean. When she pulled off of him, he ran his thumb over her lip, gathering a drop she'd missed licking, and held it for her to suck. He closed his eyes as she sucked his thumb in erotic draws.

"Enough."

Beth opened her eyes to stare up into Mason's dark ones.

Chapter Six

"What were you thinking about, Beth?"

"J–Just going over some scenes for the book."

He smiled a knowing smile, sending heat up her neck into her face. She knew she was blushing and cursed her fair skin. Her pussy was soaked, and by the look on his face, he knew it.

"Was I in that little scene, Beth?"

"What? No!" She shivered at the intense stare he leveled on her.

His eyes grew darker as he leaned forward into her space. She could smell his aftershave and underneath it, his own scent of male need. She shivered when he leaned closer and whispered in her ear.

"We can give you what you need, Beth."

She jerked back in the chair. The words haunted her. They were so close to the words on the note in the basket.

"Fuck! I'm sorry, Beth. I shouldn't have said that. Not with everything going on."

She stood up and nearly lost her balance. He caught her, and then released his hold on her when she took a step back.

"I–I think I'll take a nap before I write anymore." She quickly shut down her computer and all but ran up to the bedroom.

She shut the door and hesitated before clicking the lock in place. She didn't doubt that they would have keys to the door, but it gave her a small since of security. There was no way he could be her stalker, but he'd said almost the same thing that had been in the basket. It was just a coincidence. It had to be. Mason would never hurt her.

Beth paced the bedroom for several minutes before she finally calmed down enough to try to sleep. She pulled off her shoes but kept the rest of her clothes on. Then she climbed up on the bed and curled up to try to sleep.

Every time she closed her eyes, the contents of the basket appeared in her mind, followed by the memory of the single tail at her back. She turned over and tried again, with the same results. She wasn't going to get any sleep like this. She needed something to help her sleep. Since she didn't take sleeping pills, the only thing she could come up with was to soak in a hot bath.

She got up and ran the tub full of water, adding some of her bath salts from her bag. Then she lowered herself into the tub and sighed. It enveloped her in its warm embrace while the soft scent of vanilla soothed her nerves. She leaned back and totally submerged all but her head in the liquid heat as she closed her eyes and relaxed.

She wasn't sure how long she soaked, but when the water cooled, she sighed and climbed out of the tub. After drying off, she opened the bathroom door to find Mason sitting on the edge of her bed. Beth nearly screamed at the unexpected sight of him. She should have known he wouldn't leave her alone after she'd run from him.

"Beth, I'm sorry."

"It's okay, Mason. Um, I need to get dressed." She raised a hopeful eyebrow, but he didn't move.

"Hurry and dress, and then let's go downstairs and talk."

She drew in a deep breath and let it out slowly. Nodding her head, she rummaged around in her suitcase until she found what she needed. Then she turned her back and dressed. Once she was finished, she brushed her hair and walked through the door leaving Mason to follow.

She went straight to the fridge and pulled out a beer without asking. She had no idea what time it was since she had left her phone on the dining room table, but it didn't matter. She needed a beer.

"Beth, look at me, baby."

She took a sip of it then turned around and looked up into Mason's eyes. She could see the worry and strain in them. Part of her wanted to soothe him, and part of her wanted to run from him.

"I'm sorry, Beth. I know what I said was out of line and it reminded you of your stalker. I didn't mean to upset you."

"It's okay, Mason. I'm just jumpy."

She took another sip and turned to walk back into the dining room. She could feel Mason following her. When she sat down at the table, he took a seat across from her.

"What is the name of this book?"

The question took her by surprise, and she answered without thinking about it.

"*Everything She Needs.*" The similarities weren't lost on her. He'd said almost the exact same thing earlier. "It's the sequel to the first book. I guess whoever he is, he knows it, too. I'd talked enough about it in the office on the phone."

"Mac will get him, Beth. All of this will be over soon."

"But nothing will ever be the same again, Mason. Will it?"

He shook his head. "No."

"Because you know my secrets, too, now."

"We'll talk about it later, Beth. Go back to writing. I won't bother you. I'll be in the office if you need me." He stood up and walked out of the room.

Beth took a gulp of the beer, nearly choking on it. She set it on a coaster and opened her computer back up. It took it a few minutes to boot up. When it did, she cleared her mind and concentrated on the book.

Sometime later, the ringing of her cell phone pulled her out of her work. She frowned and checked the number. It was unlisted. She stared at it unsure what to do. Finally she answered it, but it had gone to voice mail. She waited, then dialed her voice mail and listened.

Where are you, Beth? You're not at your house, and all my little toys are gone. I miss listening to you write and watching you sleep. You're supposed to wait for me. Where are you?

Beth almost dropped the phone. She ended the call and stood there trying to decide what to do. Finally, she headed toward Mason's office. She'd promised to let them know if he called again. The door to the office was closed. She could hear the soft murmur of a voice on the other side. Should she knock? He was obviously on the phone with someone. It could be a client.

She was still standing there when the sound of the security system being reset and a door closing startled her. She nearly dropped the phone. Then Mac was walking into the living room. He saw her and frowned.

"What is it?"

"Um, he called back. I was just about to let Mason know."

"Why is his door closed?"

"He's on the phone I think. I could hear him talking."

"Give me the phone, Beth."

"He left a message."

"You listened to it." He made it a statement.

"Yes. I wanted to know what he said."

Mac hit redial and listened to the message without taking his eyes off of her. She saw the muscle in his jaw jump as he ground his teeth.

The door to the office opened and Mason walked out with a frown on his face.

"I heard voices."

"Beth got another call."

Mason's eyes jumped to her then back to Mac. "What did he say?"

Mac tossed the phone to him.

Mason frowned and listened to the message. He grimaced and handed the phone back to Mac. The two men exchanged looks, leaving Beth to wonder what that was all about.

"What have you found out so far?" Mason asked.

"Let's move this to the living room." Mac led the way.

Beth sat down on the edge of the couch. Mason sat next to her without touching her. Mac took the chair across from them.

"I've put in a call to find out if Larry is still a resident of the mental institution where they were housing him. There's a lot of red tape you have to go through to get information out of those places. I may end up needing your help, Mason. I'll let you know."

"I'll go ahead and start some paperwork so it will be ready. I need the name of the institution and anything else you know about him."

Mac nodded. "There were no fingerprints anywhere that didn't match yours, Beth. Has anyone ever been inside your house?"

"Um, I suppose not. At least not since I moved in."

He frowned. Why did that seem to make him angry? She found herself wanting to defend herself. She liked her privacy. What was wrong with that?

"What about the basket?" Mason asked.

"No prints and everything you can buy at any department store or fetish shop, including the handcuffs. I thought they were police issue, but once we examined them, they weren't. They were very good replicas, but not the real deal."

"What's next, Mac?" Mason looked disgusted that more hadn't come up.

"We're trying to see if we can trace who bought the hardware. If we can, we may have our man."

"If you can't?" she asked.

"Then we work another angle. Beth, we'll get this guy."

"When are they going to start on my security system?"

Mac exchanged looks with Mason.

"We're still processing your house, baby. Give me another day, and then we'll get them over to start on your house."

"Then I can go home." She made it a statement because she was going no matter what they said.

Mac and Mason were dangerous individuals and put them together, and they were irresistible. She wasn't strong enough to tell them no. She had wanted them for far too long to resist them should they want her.

Why does it matter? I want them, so why can't I have them? Because they would have absolute control of me and I'll never allow anyone to have that much control over me again.

"Beth, Beth?"

She looked up. Mac was talking to her.

"I'm sorry, what?"

"Have you talked to anyone today?"

"No, why?"

"So no one knows where you are."

"Um, no."

"Keep it that way. I don't want this guy to find out where you are if we can help it."

"Okay." She stood up. "I'm going to go back to writing. I'm short on my word count today."

"Go ahead, baby. We're going to be in the office if you need us." Mac stood up and nodded his head toward the office.

She shrugged and headed toward the dining room. She heard the door to the office close. Just as she stared writing again, the sound of shouts could be heard coming from the general direction of the office. She winced. They were fighting, and she was sure it was concerning her.

A few minutes later, the door opened. She ignored them and continued writing. It wasn't until Mac walked in with a plate that she realized how much time had passed. She looked up.

"Time to eat."

"Just set it down. I'll eat when I've finished this chapter."

"You can put your muses on hold long enough to eat, Beth." It was a statement, not a question.

"I suppose." She wasn't happy about it, but didn't want to cause any more trouble than she already had.

Mac disappeared into the kitchen only to return with another plate and joined her. She didn't look up. Instead, she concentrated on her plate and eating.

"How's the new book coming?"

"I'm on track for the most part."

"Mason tells me that you, um, had an interesting conversation earlier. You freaked out. Do you want to talk about it?"

"Not especially."

"I think it pertains to this case, Beth. What scared you? Was it Mason or what he said?"

She toyed with her fork then licked her suddenly dry lips.

"He said almost exactly the same words as is in the title of my book. Plus, they were close to what the stalker said on that note. The stalker knows what I'm writing, because he would have heard it when I was talking to my agent on the phone."

"You know Mason isn't the stalker, don't you, Beth?"

"I–I guess."

Mac sighed and sat back in the chair. He placed both hands flat on the table and stood up. Beth leaned back in her chair as he did. She couldn't help her reaction to him. He was so big. He reached out to touch her. When she jerked in the chair, he sighed.

"You're scared of both of us, aren't you, Beth?"

"You're just so big, Mac, and you represent everything I left behind thinking I would never deal with it again. The closest I ever wanted to get to it again was in my books."

"We'd never hurt you, Beth. If you don't believe anything else, believe that. No matter what else happens, know that you can always depend on either one of us to help you."

Beth could only nod her head. She didn't think she could speak a word if her life depended on it. It was all too much too fast. She stood up and took the plates and carried them to the kitchen. Mason was eating alone at the bar. When she walked in, he looked unsure of whether he should stay or go.

She smiled shyly at him before cleaning off the dishes and putting them in the dishwasher. Then she returned to the dining room, now empty of Mac. She took her seat and began writing once again. The words were flowing much too fast for her to keep up as she frantically typed.

Sometime later, Mason stepped into the room and cleared his throat. She ignored him as she filled her computer screen with words. Finally he shook his head and left. A few minutes later, Mac walked in. He didn't waste time trying to get her attention. He merely snapped her laptop closed.

"Hey! I'll lose what I'm working on!"

"Then save it, and come to bed. You're not working all night. You've got to be in good shape with a stalker hanging around. I'm not going to let you wear yourself out staying up all night writing. Now save the fucking book, and come on."

Beth pouted but saved her work and powered off the computer. Then she grabbed her phone and winced at the time on it. It was 1:00 a.m. No wonder he was a bit miffed. He had to get up the next morning, whereas she could sleep in if she wanted to.

He followed her upstairs and into the bedroom. She stopped dead still when she saw Mason in boxers, silk boxers, climbing into bed. *Aw, hell.*

She turned to tell Mac that she couldn't sleep with them only to find him stripping out of his uniform. She stood mesmerized by the sight of his magnificent body. Everything from his broad chest to the defined muscles of his calves screamed primal male. Then there was that tattoo on his bicep. Mac was a beautiful specimen of a male.

"Beth? Are you going to get dressed for bed? Do you need help, baby?"

"No! I mean, I can do it myself."

She located her sleep shirt and hid in the bathroom for as long as she dared. Then she walked back out to find the lights out except for a bedside lamp on Mac's side. When she approached the bed, Mac was sitting there waiting for her.

"Come on and get in bed. You're bound to be exhausted. You've been up a long time."

"I'm used to it. I'll write nonstop for several days then crash for a few days. It's the way I'm used to writing. I don't know how forcing me to go to sleep is going to affect my writing."

Mac shook his head and pulled back the cover, indicating she should climb under them. Beth frowned but got into the bed and scooted over to the center of the bed. She managed to keep from touching either man when Mac lay down next to her. He turned off the light.

The last thing Beth remembered thinking about was how she was going to manage to forget Mac and Mason when everything went back to normal. She would have to do it. She wasn't able to be who they needed. She wasn't that woman anymore.

Chapter Seven

Mac woke up the next morning with Beth asleep on top of him. He grinned. No doubt she was going to be embarrassed when she woke up. He waited for as long as he could before he woke her up. He enjoyed her body being in such close proximity to hers. No doubt she wouldn't appreciate it one bit.

"Beth, baby? Wake up. I have to get up and go to work."

She moaned and stretched before hugging him tighter. He smiled. She was so cute when she was asleep. The little dainty snore and the way she moved all combined to make her so special. He tried again.

"Beth, you need to get up. Wake up, baby." He poked her in the ribs.

"Hey!" She growled at him, and then opened her eyes.

"Oh. My. God. I'm sorry, Mac. I–I'll get down."

"It's all right. Just be careful getting off of me."

He grunted when she rolled off of him toward the center of the bed and into Mason.

"What?"

"I'm sorry, Mason. See, you really shouldn't sleep with me. I'm dangerous."

"Go back to sleep. I'm not going into the office for another few hours." Mason rolled over on top of her and was snoring again in no time.

"Mac, you've got to help me. I need to get up."

"Talk to Mason, Beth. He's usually reasonable if you have a good reason." He grinned down at her and headed for his bedroom so he could get dressed.

He wanted to push a little harder on finding out if Larry was still locked away, or if he'd been released. Then he would know to focus on something else. Right now, he had zip. And that made him very uneasy.

He walked downstairs to start some coffee. Expecting to have to make it, he was puzzled to find the coffeemaker already working. Mason must have already gotten up. He heard a noise in the dining room and froze. He flipped the snap off his holster and kept his hand on his gun as he slipped to the side of the door leading into the room. He eased around the edge of the doorway and stopped, closing his eyes. He took his hand off his gun and stepped back.

Beth was sitting at the table totally immersed in whatever she was writing. It never registered with her that she was in danger. Mac backed away and returned to the kitchen to calm down. Then he shook his head and smiled. How had she managed to get out from under Mason without the other man being down there with her?

He poured two cups of coffee and carried them into the dining room. He waited for her to look up and notice that he was bringing her coffee. When she didn't look up, he cleared his throat.

"Hi Mac." She still didn't look up.

"I've got coffee."

"Thanks. Just sit it on the coaster." She did look up for a second, and then she was back typing.

"Where is Mason?"

"Hmm? Oh, he's still in bed."

"I'm leaving, Beth. Don't open the door to anyone. Get Mason if someone rings the bell."

"Okay."

He wasn't at all sure any of it had gotten through to her. She needed a keeper if this was how she got while she was writing. Well, as soon as they got passed the stalker problem, they would work on her.

He left her in the dining room pecking away at the computer. He poured coffee into a thermos and locked up the house behind him after resetting the alarm system. He would call Mason later and find out how she managed to get away from him.

Mac pulled up at the diner and noticed a strange car in the parking lot. He'd never seen it before. It had Texas plates, but a different county. He made note of it but didn't call it in right away. He wanted to get a look at whoever was driving it first.

When he walked inside, Mattie was standing behind the counter talking to a customer. He looked around and located the stranger in the back drinking coffee and reading a paper. He was of average height, about two fifty pounds and had sandy-blond hair. He was roughly thirty-one or two and had blue eyes. He took his usual position at the counter and waited for Mattie to make her way over.

"Hey, Mac, how are you doing this morning? Want your usual?" Mattie started to pour him a cup of coffee.

Mac shook his head and put his hand over his cup.

"I need a to-go order today, Mattie. How's everything going?"

"Doing fine. Nothing going on around here."

"What about the stranger in the back?"

"Oh, he's been in a couple of days now. Said he's looking at buying some property around here."

"Any other strangers that you've noticed lately?"

"What's going on, Mac? Anything I need to know about?"

"No, just trying to keep up with the town. We've had a rash of newcomers here lately."

"Well, that's the only new person I've seen lately. I'll ask my waitresses to let me know if they serve anyone new." She smiled and headed for the window to the back to call in his order.

Mac walked around the diner, stopping to talk to various people as he slowly made his way to the stranger in the back. When he stopped in front of the man's table, he looked up from the paper and smiled.

"Something I can help you with, Officer?"

"Just being friendly and a little nosey. My name is Mac Tidwell."
He held out his hand to the other man.

"Bob Jones. Nice to meet you." He shook Mac's hand with an
easy, firm handshake.

Mac couldn't find fault in it or the way the man responded. He
was probably who he said he was, but Mac was naturally suspicious.
He took a seat without asking if he could join the man and sipped his
coffee.

"What brings you to Riverbend?"

"Looking at some property out this way. Thought I'd look around
and see how I like it here."

"Where are you looking? There's not that much for sale around
here."

"They call it the McGovern's place. Nice little house with twenty-
five acres. I'm thinking about keeping horses."

"Place has been for sale for several years. Have you seen the
house yet? It's in pretty bad shape."

"Nothing a little work won't put to rights." He grinned, and Mac's
instincts kicked into overdrive.

He stood up and nodded. "Enjoy your stay. I'm at the sheriff's
office if you need any help."

"Why thank you, Officer."

Mac didn't bother correcting him. The man was slimy. He didn't
know what it was, but he wasn't looking at the McGovern's place to
start up a horse ranch. It would take a lot more than a little work to
make that house livable. Last time he'd been out that direction the
roof was caving in.

He walked back toward the register where Mattie was waiting
with his order. He paid and walked back to his truck, making a mental
note to check with the local reality company to see how much of the
man's story was true. Something about the man smelled off. He didn't
know what it was, yet. But he would find out.

Once he reached the office, he made a few quick calls to scope out the man's story. Then he got down to the business of the day answering messages and checking reports. He had four other deputies on staff with a secretary during the day and a dispatcher at night. He called up to his secretary's desk.

"Connie, have you heard anything back from that call I had you make yesterday to the Quiet Hands Mental Hospital?"

"No sir. I did get an answer to the question about The Dungeon in Dallas. I put it on your desk under all of the phone messages."

He sighed and dug through the stack of reports to find the message stack. There it was at the bottom of the stack like she said. He never would have gotten to it without asking her. She tried, but she was a nervous little thing. Nothing he'd done had made her feel any more comfortable around the station.

Putting her out of his mind, he read the note and cursed. Another roadblock. They wouldn't give out information on their clients without a court order. He had known better but had hoped to catch a break there.

He checked his watch and realized it was close to lunchtime, and he hadn't called Mason or checked on Beth. He quickly dialed Mason's cell. After the third ring, he answered.

"Mac, she's a fucking contortionist."

"So she just slipped out from under you, huh?"

"Something like that. What's up?"

"I'm not getting anywhere right now, and it's pissing me off. What was she doing when you left?"

"Writing. She totally ignored me when I ate breakfast at the dining room table."

"I need you to start work on pushing for information from that hospital that Larry is in. I can't get any answers from anyone there. We need to know so we can rule him out and look for someone closer to home."

Mac heard shuffling papers in the background then Mason said, "Go ahead."

"Quiet Hands in San Antonio. I talked with a Dr. Harry Brown yesterday. He was going to check with his superiors to see if they could release any information like that to us. I faxed them the request on official letterhead, but it's not going anywhere. See what you can do."

"I'll get started on it. I'll let you know when I find anything out."

"I'll swing by the house for lunch and check on Beth," Mac told him.

"Good. I was going to, but this will give me more time to do some searching."

They hung up, and Mac snapped his phone back on his belt. He made one more phone call and found out that the stranger actually had been looking at the property, but that the owner refused to sell to him when he made a ridiculously low offer. Mac smiled. The property was held in trust by the mayor. Since the mayor wanted to keep his job and his town free of bigotry, he would make sure only someone approved by the city council would be able to buy that land.

Satisfied that at least that was taken care of, Mac stood up and headed toward the front of the office.

"I'm going to run by the house for lunch today, Connie. Call me if you need me."

"Will do." She quickly looked down and kept typing.

It reminded him of Beth. Suddenly, he needed to be there. He hurried out the door and fired up the truck even before he had his seat belt on. When he turned down their private road, he passed a car with darkly tinted windows speeding away. He couldn't read the plates. They were covered with something. He cursed but continued toward the house. He needed to see that Beth was okay.

Mac screeched to a halt in the drive and jumped out of the truck, taking the steps at a dead run. He quickly unlocked the door and hit the alarm as he ran toward the dining room. She wasn't there. He checked the living room, but she wasn't there either. Finally, he checked the bedroom and found her lying facedown on the bed as if she'd fallen there.

His throat closed up in fear. He hurried over to the bed and checked her pulse. It was strong and steady. Then he carefully turned her over and her eyes flew open with a scream.

"Hey! Hey, Beth. It's just me."

"What are you doing waking me up? I was sleeping just fine."

"You were flat on your face. How can you breathe sleeping like that?"

"I sleep like I want to, and you can sleep like you want to." She glared up at him.

"You scared me to death. I passed someone on the road speeding away and thought something had happened to you."

She sobered. "I'm sorry. I'm fine though. No one's been here."

"Come on downstairs. I'm going to fix sandwiches for lunch. Then I'm going to look around outside to see if anyone's been sneaking around."

Beth followed him downstairs toward the kitchen. She helped him pull together the sandwiches and managed to eat one entire sandwich.

"That's all I can eat. You'll have to eat the other one, or I can save it for later."

"Wrap it up and eat it later. Dinner will probably be a little later tonight. Mason is working on his case, and I have some paperwork in the office to work on first."

"I'd cook, but I'm not very good at it. I usually eat microwave or order pizza."

"That's okay, Beth. You don't have to cook while you're here. One of us will do it as soon as we can." He wiped a smear of mayo off the corner of her mouth and licked it with a smile. "I'm going to look around before I leave. Stay inside and don't…"

"Answer the door for anyone or my phone unless I know who it is," she finished for him.

"Good girl." He disarmed the alarm and checked it before rearming it and locking the door behind him.

Once outside, he began walking around the house, looking for any evidence that someone had been snooping around. He found one small area near the dining room where someone had stood. At that position, if he were tall enough, he could see inside the dining room if the blinds were open, like they were now. He cursed and returned to the truck. He dialed Beth's cell phone. She finally answered on the fourth ring.

"Mac?"

"Why did you open the blinds, baby?"

"To get more light in the room. It's dark in your house."

He sighed. "Close them for me, Beth. Someone was looking in that window."

"Oh, God. Do I need to go somewhere else? He knows I'm here now."

"Shh, Beth. Calm down, and listen to me. He can't get in the house if you don't let him in. Keep the doors locked, and the alarm will trigger at the police station and the sheriff's office if he tries to get in. You'll be safe."

"Are you sure?"

"I'm sure. I'll be home as soon as I can, baby. Stay put, and close those damn blinds."

"I'm closing them now. Oh, God."

He could hear the panic in her voice. He wanted her a little scared so she would follow directions, but he didn't want her in a panic. She would make a mistake that way. He continued to talk to her in a calm voice until she was breathing normal and sounded more like herself.

"Okay. I'm going to hang up now. Call me if you need me."

He snapped the phone back on his belt and headed back to the office. He needed some answers, and he needed them yesterday.

Chapter Eight

Beth steadied her breathing and put down the phone. She double-checked every blind and drape in the house. Once she was sure they were all closed, she returned to the dining room and tried to get back into writing, but the urge was no longer there. Instead, she was restless, and she couldn't go anywhere.

She walked around the house, not really suspicious but curious and antsy. She found the locked room off the kitchen that had obviously been the carport at one time. She speculated what was behind the locked door until she was making wild guesses like a bat cave where they transformed into superheroes at night.

She found herself back in the kitchen and nowhere near settled down. She sighed and decided on a cup of coffee. She set the coffee to brew and thought about Larry for the first time in a long time. She often wondered if she should have seen what was happening in him. Had it been her fault that he had snapped? The Masters had said it had nothing to do with her. That he had probably always had a deep-seated problem that stayed just below the surface.

Had she been so wrapped up in herself back then that she hadn't seen the signs that something was wrong? Surely there had been signs. Thinking back, she could remember little things, such as his unusual anger at the mailman for leaving the mailbox door open. Had that been a signal she had missed?

For those short months, she had thought she might have found someone she could fall in love with. Looking back now, she realized that if she were going to fall for him, she would have before then.

She poured a cup of the coffee and took it into the living room where she curled up on the sofa in hopes of relaxing. Her phone rang in the other room. She almost didn't get up to check it, but she set the coffee down and hurried to the dining room. It was Mason.

"Hello?"

"Why did it take you so long to answer the phone?"

"I was in the living room, and the phone was in the dining room."

"You need to keep it with you all the time, baby. You never know where you'll be and need it."

She could hear the strain in Mason's voice. He was worried about her and had the trial coming up as well.

"I will, Mason. I wasn't thinking."

"Mac told me that someone was hanging around at the house. Did you close all the blinds?"

"Don't worry. I did that first thing. I even closed the ones upstairs."

"Good girl. I'll be late coming home. Stay safe for me."

"Bye, Mason." She hit *end* and slipped the phone in her pocket before walking back to the living room.

She picked up her coffee again and sipped at it as she let her mind wander. Before she knew it, she was back at the dining room table writing. Back on track, she put everything else behind her until her eyes began to water and she needed a bathroom break. She pulled out her phone to check the time. It was nearly six. Where was everyone? She hurried upstairs to the bathroom then back downstairs to check the office. Mac wasn't there.

Should she call one of them or just wait for them to come home? They had said they would be late, but how late was late to them? Beth unwrapped her sandwich and ate it as she worried about the men. She was sure they were okay.

It hit her that she was worried about two men she had promised herself she wouldn't get involved with. With a groan, she realized that it was too late. She was already involved with them. They'd already pushed their way into her life and now were working on her heart.

She returned to the dining room and sat behind the computer to stare at the screen. She couldn't be who they needed. She didn't have the ability to trust that completely again. Mac and Mason lived the life and wouldn't be able to survive without it. She couldn't turn over control to someone ever again. It just wasn't in her anymore.

She had no doubt that they were going to try to talk her into it. She might even try, but they'd see her failure to trust them as personal. She didn't want them to think that she didn't trust them specifically, but trust just didn't come easily for her anymore. It was why she didn't really have friends, just acquaintances.

Friends required a lot of time and personal sacrifice. She couldn't handle that anymore. When one betrayed you, it hurt to the quick. Beth wouldn't risk it again, so she didn't make friends.

Before she realized it, she was writing again and the alarm was beeping. She immediately got up and grabbed her cell phone. Then she hid behind the door, waiting to see what would happen.

"Beth?" Mac's voice resounded throughout the lower floor.

She hurried into the kitchen. He smiled when he saw her. She couldn't help throwing herself into his arms.

"The alarm was beeping? Why. You always turn it off before it beeps."

"I'm sorry, baby. I had my hands full. I brought Chinese takeout for dinner. I hope you like Chinese."

"I love it. Where's Mason?"

"He's going to be late tonight. They had something come up in the case. How has the writing been?"

She sighed. "Off and on. I got spooked earlier, and it took a while to get back into it."

"No phone calls?"

"Just Mason."

"Okay, let's eat before it gets cold. Mason can warm his back up when he gets in."

They ate in silence. Beth could tell Mac wanted to talk about something, but he was biding his time. She didn't like waiting, so she started the conversation instead.

"What's bothering you, Mac?"

He sighed and put down his chopsticks. "I'm having trouble finding out if Larry is still in that hospital. Mason is working on it, but I don't like waiting. Do you have someone you can contact to check on him?"

"Um, maybe. I kept in touch with the Masters for a while, but I haven't talked to them in over a year now. I don't even know if the phone number still works."

"Was it in your cell phone?"

"No, it's on my computer. I didn't keep it there in case my phone ever got stolen. It's their private number."

"It's only nine. Can you call them now?" Mac asked.

Beth nodded and carried her phone over to her computer. She pulled up her directory and found the phone number and dialed it. It rang three times before Master James answered.

"Beth, how are you doing?"

"I'm well, Master James. I'm sorry to call so late, but I need some help."

"What can I do for you?"

"Do you know if Larry is out or not?"'

There was silence on the other end of the phone. She started to ask if he was still there, but he finally answered her.

"I don't know, Beth. Is something wrong?"

"Someone is stalking me, and the sheriff here is trying to see if he's still in the hospital or not. No one will tell them anything. Do you have some way to find out?"

"I'll talk to Master Williams and we'll see what we can do. Are you safe, Beth? You can always come here if you need a safe place to stay for a while."

"Thank you, Master James, but I'm in a safe place."

"We'll find out what we can and call you back at this number."

She thanked him again and hung up. When she turned around, Mac's face had gone stone cold. She shivered.

"Martin James and Henry Williams?"

"You know them?"

"We're acquainted." He didn't say anything else.

"They're going to let me know what they find out."

"Beth, did they ever top you?"

"Why, Mac? Why does it matter?"

"Just answer the question, Beth."

"Yes, Mac. In class they topped me."

"Only in class?"

"Only in class."

Mac seemed to release a breath he'd been holding. Then he was all business again.

"Finish your meal."

"I'm not hungry anymore." She got up and took the rest of her food and stored it in the fridge.

She returned to the dining room and sat back in front of the computer. She would write. It always helped. Mac remained sitting at the table staring at her. She felt like something major had happened, and she wasn't privy to what it was. It threw her off. She fiddled around with the keys for a while then finally got up and started to walk out of the room.

"Where are you going?"

"To take a shower. I'm tired. I think I'm going to go on to bed."

"I'll shut everything down and come up with you." Mac started to get up.

"No, Mac. I'm going to shower by myself and go to bed—by myself."

His jaw worked, but he nodded a quick nod and followed her into the living room. She could feel him watching her as she climbed the stairs. Once alone, she hurried with her shower and climbed into bed to try and sleep. Instead, she thought about everything that had happened and wondered what she would do if Larry had gotten out.

* * * *

Mac waited until Mason got home around ten that night. The other man lifted an eyebrow when he saw him sitting in the living room with the lights off nursing a shot of whiskey.

"Bad day at the office?"

"You could say that. How's the case coming? He's not going to get off is he?"

"No, he's not getting off. Tell me what's going on."

"I got impatient and had Beth call someone to find out if Larry had made it out or not."

"And?"

"She called one of her old Masters. They're going to see if they can find out and let her know."

"So why the whiskey and the dangerous glint in your eye?"

"Her Masters in Dallas were Martin James and Henry Williams."

"Son of a bitch!"

Mason walked over to the fireplace and leaned against it for a few seconds before turning around and heading toward where they stashed the whiskey. Mac watched him pour two fingers and down it. Then he poured a little more and put the bottle away.

"Did they top her, Mac? Because I know you asked."

"In class, but never outside of class."

"Does she know anything?"

"No."

"Fuck!"

Mac drained his whiskey and leaned back against the back of the couch. He closed his eyes and willed his anger under control. Seeing Mason upset only brought his anger back out in force. His brother had cared about Julia a little more than he had, but Mac had still cared.

It was before Beth. She hadn't been in the picture yet. They topped Julia for nearly a year when she had gone to Dallas to spend the weekend with some of her college friends. When she came back, she was a different person. She finally confessed to them that she had gone to a club there in Dallas and met Martin and Henry. They had talked her into a scene, and she'd been drinking too much. She'd agreed. Nothing happened out of the ordinary, but she'd fallen in love with them. When she went back, they ignored her and said they weren't interested, that she'd been fine for one time.

She went back to Dallas to see them again and never made it back home. She wrecked her car on the way back. She'd been drinking, something she had never done when they'd been together. Once the pieces had been put together, they discovered she'd had a fight with an unknown boyfriend and left the club crying. Mason had blamed himself and withdrawn until that day in July when they'd hit on Beth.

"What are the fucking odds, Mac? What are the fucking odds?"

"I know, Mason. She isn't in love with them. She hasn't even talked to them in over a year 'til tonight."

"They'll be calling back."

"I know. I'm the one who had her call the bastards."

"Hell, Mac. You didn't know." Mason drank the rest of his whiskey and sat down across from him.

"What are we going to do?"

"I guess that all depends on Beth. She's ultimately the one who has the last say."

"I hope they don't call without one of us here with her. I don't trust them."

"You can always make her go to the office with you."

"Except I'm not always there. Mick is out sick, and Lamar is on vacation."

"I can't stay with this case heating up like it is. She's safe as long as she stays here in the house."

Mac knew he was right, but he didn't like it. This guy was sophisticated. He knew his way around electronics. If something happened to Beth...Nothing could happen to her, and that was that. He'd make stops by the house as much as possible. Somehow, they had to keep her safe. Even if it was as much from herself as it was from her stalker.

Chapter Nine

Beth moaned as she dreamed that Mac was licking her belly while Mason sucked on her nipples. Neither man had said anything, just come to bed and attacked her. She knew it had to be a dream, because it felt too good to be real.

Her dream lovers kissed and licked all over her body. Mac continued down her abdomen to her pelvis. He ran his tongue in a swirling motion around her ticklish spots at the tops of her groin. She couldn't stop the little whimpers that escaped her mouth. The feel of his tongue on her skin sent shivers down her spine.

Mason nipped at her nipples before laving them with his tongue to soothe the pain. When he drew one into his mouth and sucked it tight against the roof of his mouth, she shivered all over. He teased it then released it to capture the other one, treating it to the same devastating effects.

She whimpered when Mac settled between her legs, pushing them apart to accommodate his wide shoulders. He blew on her pussy lips then licked them and sucked them inside his mouth to play. The sensation felt too real. She opened her eyes and would have cried out, except that Mac chose that instant to lick over her clit with the flat of his tongue. What were they doing to her?

"She's awake, Mac. Our little Beth is wide awake." Mason nipped at one of her nipples, earning him a yelp.

"I hear her." Mac continued licking along her slit.

Her juices were flowing freely now with all the stimulation. Never had she been so excited and turned on before. No one had ever aroused even half the feelings she had flowing through her blood now. They were devastating. If she let them make love to her, she would never be the same again.

Mac spread her pussy lips and lapped at her like a kitten after milk. Then he entered her cunt with two fingers and pumped them in and out of her. All reason left her, and any thought of sending them away vanished.

"You taste like apple cider, all tart and sweet at the same time. I'll never get enough of you, Beth." Mac circled her clit with the tip of his tongue.

It had her pussy contracting around his fingers as he speared her with them. He curled his fingers inside of her and found that special spot in a woman that sent them over the moon.

"Oh, God!" She bowed her back. It felt so good.

Mason continued teasing and tormenting her breasts. He licked over one nipple while he pinched or pulled on the other one. The pleasure-pain sent spears of desire straight to her clit. All it would take was one suck of Mac's mouth on it to send her flying. She fought it, knowing that it was useless but doing it anyway. She couldn't afford to climax. It would damn her for sure. She would never be able to get them out of her system.

Mac used one hand to hold her down as he continued fucking her with his fingers. He licked up and down her slit from his fingers to her clit. When she didn't think she could take anymore, he sucked in her clit and tapped it over and over with his tongue. Mason twisted her nipples, sending even more stimulation to her clit. She exploded. Her body was no longer her own as she screamed out their names. They had sent her somewhere she had never been before, and Beth was sure she would never be the same again.

Fire burned along her nerves and in her blood as Mac slowly brought her down. He kissed her pussy and all along her inner thighs as Mason whispered in her ear. His words didn't make sense at first until she could truly hear through the ringing in her ears. He told her how pretty she was when she came and how good she'd done. Over and over he praised her as he kissed along her neck and jaw.

Finally, Mac crawled up her body and lay next to her on the opposite side of Mason. He ran the back of his hand over her cheek before leaning in and kissing her.

She could taste the evidence of her passion on his lips. It wasn't an unpleasant taste as he pushed his tongue into her mouth and explored it. He slid alongside hers before licking his way around inside. She moaned, unable to fight him, not wanting to fight him anymore. Something inside of her knew that there was no running from them now. She would belong to them before it was over with.

Finally, Mac pulled back, and Mason nipped at her lower lip before delving into her mouth with his tongue. She whimpered. He licked and sucked on hers before pulling back and kissing the corners of her mouth.

Both men stared down at her with enough passion in their eyes to scare her. They wanted her, and she couldn't say no. Instead of pressing their need on her, they pulled the covers back up over her. Mac pulled her back into his arms, spooning her so that she faced Mason. Mason gave her one last kiss before turning and backing up to her. She had no choice but to drape her arm over his back. She didn't want it anywhere else. She knew she was right where she wanted to be.

* * * *

Mason slipped out of bed early the next morning to get an early start so maybe he could come home at a decent hour that night. He hated leaving Beth alone for so long with a stalker out there looking for her. He knew Mac would swing by several times during the day, but it wasn't enough as far as Mason was concerned.

Then there was the idea that Martin or Henry would probably be calling her back sometime during the day. He didn't trust them. They had known what they were doing when they had lured Julia into their hands. They knew she had been vulnerable, but it hadn't mattered to them. Mac and Mason had confronted them about it after Julia's death, and they swore it hadn't been like that.

The two men said they didn't realize how submissive she was until they did the scene, and by then it was too late. She'd placed her focus on them. They tried to reason with her, but she hadn't listened and ran. Mason couldn't believe that being Masters they wouldn't know how vulnerable she was. He just didn't believe them.

Mason dressed and walked downstairs to fix coffee. He didn't feel like cooking this morning. When he finished, he grabbed his briefcase and headed toward the door. He heard a sound behind him and turned around to find Beth standing there looking uncomfortable.

"Hey, baby. Did you need something?"

"No. I was coming down to fix coffee and saw you leaving."

"Call me if you need anything, Beth. I mean it. And don't answer the phone for anyone you don't know."

"I won't. I know the drill." She huffed out a breath and turned toward the coffeepot.

Mason felt like he had failed some test of hers. He didn't even know what it was about. He stood there a few seconds then turned and left. She would be fine, he told himself several times on the way to the office.

Once he reached his desk, the case pulled at him until he was immersed in it once again. It wasn't until nearly ten thirty that he realized he hadn't called to check on Beth. He cursed and made the call. When she didn't answer, he panicked. He stood up, getting ready to go see about her when his cell phone rang. He answered it without looking at who was calling.

"Yeah."

"Did you just call me, Mason?"

"Where were you? I was worried." He sat back down with an inward sigh and ran a hand over his face.

"Sorry. I ran up to the bathroom and left my phone on the table by the computer. I never dreamed anyone would call while I was gone for less than two minutes."

"Keep the phone with you all the time, Beth. You never know when you might need it."

"I will. Did you need something?"

"I was just checking to see if you were doing all right."

He heard her sigh over the phone. "I'm fine. I'm writing. No one has called, and no one has knocked on the door. I have all the drapes and blinds closed. Don't worry about me, Mason. I'm safe here. You told me it was the best security system money could buy."

"It is, baby, but nothing is perfect. I can't help but worry."

"Don't. Go back to work, Mason. You have an important trial to prepare for. I have a deadline to make." She ended the call before he could say anything more.

Mason shook his head and laid his phone back on the desk. There was nothing he could do but trust that she would be fine. It was hard to do that when he cared a little too much for her already. They had been steering clear of her for so long that he had forgotten just how much of a punch in the gut it was to be near her. The night before had sealed her fate as far as he was concerned. She was theirs, and he would do everything in his power to keep her safe.

His cell phone rang again. He checked the number. It was Mac. He quickly answered it.

"Yeah."

"Were you just on the phone with Beth?"

"Yeah, why?"

"I tried to call, and it went straight to voice mail. I was afraid of who she might be talking to. If it was you, I won't call her 'til later. I may just swing by at lunch unless I have to answer a call."

"Sounds good. I'll check on her again this afternoon. I don't like not knowing anything, Mac."

"I know. I'm doing the best that I can. So far, we don't have anything to work with. No fingerprints, no footprints clear enough to make a cast. He's sophisticated enough to know his way around electronics and smart enough to keep under the radar. It's going to be hard to catch him, Mason. Damn hard."

"Fuck! There has to be some way to get him out in the open so we can nail his ass."

"I've got to go. I'll keep in touch."

Mason pressed *end* and held the phone in his hands as he pressed them to his forehead. He didn't have a good feeling about this one bit.

Someone knocked on his door, and he was thrown back into the case. He didn't think about calling her again until late that afternoon.

* * * *

Beth looked up when the security system beeped. She held her breath until Mac called out for her. She released it in a whoosh as she got up and headed toward the kitchen.

"I'm right here. What are you doing home?"

"It's lunchtime. I do get to eat occasionally." He flicked her nose with a finger then stole a kiss before she could back away.

She shivered. All it took was for him to be in the same room with her to send her senses reeling. Him or Mason, for that matter. They were both equally destructive.

"Oh, I didn't realize it was that late. I've been busy. How about you?" She settled on a barstool at the bar and watched as he pulled sandwiches out of a paper bag.

"It's been steady, but not too busy."

"You must have gone by the diner. How is Mattie doing?" She pulled her sandwich toward her and unwrapped it.

"She was busy when I picked up the order. It's good that business is booming, but she needs another waitress. Hers keep getting married."

Beth chuckled and smiled. Then she took a bite out of her sandwich and they ate in silence. As soon as she was finished, she cleared away the wrappers.

"Thanks for lunch. I probably wouldn't have stopped for several hours. I tend to forget the time when I'm writing and it's flowing well." She picked up her drink and headed toward the dining room.

Mac followed her as she set the drink on a coaster and took her seat. She looked up expectantly. She really needed for him to go back to work. He was distracting, and after last night, she wasn't very comfortable around him or Mason. Her emotions were too raw to deal with at the moment.

"Have you had any phone calls?"

"No, not other than Mason. He called this morning around ten or so."

Mac was about to reply when her cell phone rang. She hesitated with her hand over it before picking it up.

"Don't answer it unless you know who it is, Beth."

She looked at the number and smiled. "It's Master Williams."

Mac's face changed to one of stone. She hated seeing that side of him. He was so hard looking then.

"Okay. We need to find out what he knows. Answer it."

She frowned at him, but answered the phone.

"Hello?"

"Beth. How are you?"

"I'm doing fine. Were you able to find out anything?"

"I'm afraid it's not good news, Beth. Larry is out. They released him about a month ago."

Beth felt her blood sink to her feet. She grabbed the table for support and looked up at Mac. She knew he could tell the answer by her face. She doubted there was an ounce of color on it right then.

"Beth? Beth, are you there?"

"Yes, I'm here. I was supposed to be notified when he was released."

"I know, but you know how things work. Someone lost the paperwork or it's sitting at the bottom of a pile of papers. Are you safe, Beth?"

"I'm as safe as I can be. I'm staying with the sheriff and his brother."

There was silence on the other end of the phone. Then the strained voice of Henry returned.

"Beth, I really think you should come here and let us take care of you. We know Larry and what he's capable of. Can you say that of your sheriff? Let us keep you safe."

"I'm fine where I am, Master Williams. Thank you so much for your help. I really appreciate it."

"If you need our help, let us know, Beth. We'll come and get you if need be."

She smiled. They had always been so supportive of her. They had wanted to take her on as a submissive, but they wanted a twenty-four-seven submissive. She didn't want that kind of life. They hadn't pushed it at the time.

She said good-bye and ended the call. She looked up and could tell that Mac wasn't happy.

"He wanted you to go there, didn't he?"

"They are worried about me, Mac. I told him I was safe here with you."

"I wish you hadn't told him where you were staying. Anyone could be listening over a scanner with the right frequency and heard where you were."

She shivered. "I didn't think about that. I'm sorry."

"Hell." He looked up and drew in a deep breath.

Beth wasn't sure what was going on, but she could tell that Mac was upset. She hadn't realized that someone might overhear her on the phone. She would be more careful next time.

"Just be careful what you say, baby. I don't want to tip the man off and have him watching you here."

She didn't want that either. In fact, she wanted him to disappear and never come back. She knew that wasn't about to happen, though. She wasn't thinking, and that was dangerous. When she was in the middle of a book, she tended to put everything out of her mind but the book. She would be so focused on it that she forgot what day it was and, sometimes, to eat for several days.

"Are you going to be home late tonight?"

"I hope not. Mason said he was going to try to get home earlier, but I wouldn't count on it. His trial is tomorrow."

"I was thinking about cooking. If you're not sure, I better wait until after the trial so both of you can be here at the same time."

"There's no need for you to cook, baby. We can cook, and you're our guest."

"More like your unwilling prisoner," she muttered.

"You're not a prisoner."

"I might as well be one. I can't leave here, and I have to keep all the blinds closed. I can't answer the door or my phone unless it's one of you or someone else I know. That sounds pretty prisonerish to me."

Mac sighed and shook his head. "I'll be home as soon as I can, Beth. Don't cook. I'll cook when I get here unless Mason makes it home first. Then he can cook instead." Mac smiled the first truly genuine, full-face smile she'd seen on him since she had first seen him on her doorstep earlier in the week.

Beth didn't bother getting up to see him out. He knew his way around his own house. She heard the beep, beep of the alarm as he reset it, and the soft snap of the door closing behind him. A few seconds later, she heard the motor of his truck roar to life. She resisted the urge to run to the window and watch him leave. Part of her wanted him back. It was the part that he and Mason had uncovered the night before. The part of her that would forever belong to them.

Chapter Ten

The words flowed faster than ever before as she struggled on the computer to keep up with them. When Mason walked in the room, she screamed and nearly knocked over her drink.

"Damn! What are you doing home? Mac just left."

"He's been here since lunch?"

"Lunch? What time is it?"

"It's six o'clock, Beth. Do you always lose track of time like this?" He walked over and squatted next to her.

"Sometimes," she hedged.

"Beth, this is no way to live, baby. You need to have some sort of life outside of writing."

"Don't tell me how to live, Mason. I'm perfectly happy like I am. I don't need you telling me I'm not." She started to say more, but her phone rang.

She stared at it for a second before she picked it up. When she checked the number, it was unlisted. She looked up at Mason. He must have seen it in her eyes.

"Put it on speaker, Beth."

She answered the phone, putting it on speaker when she did.

"Hello?"

"You can't hide from me, Beth. I'll find you, and I'll give you everything you need. I know what you need, Beth. I've always known what you needed." The phone went dead.

Beth pushed *end* with a shaky hand then leaned back in the chair and closed her eyes. Mason pulled her out of the chair into his arms and held her. He didn't say anything. He just held her and ran a hand up and down her arm. Finally, she pushed away.

"I think I'm going to take a bath before I eat. I'll be back downstairs in a little while." She saved her work and closed down the computer before heading for the stairs.

She didn't think she could deal with much more. Between the men pressing her and the stalker, she felt like she was losing her sense of self. How could she resist them while she was staying with them? They would smother her and try to change her. She didn't want to change. She liked her life like it was. Sure, she missed some of the camaraderie of friends, but her writing never let her down. It was always there when she needed it.

She was sure a psychiatrist would have a field day with her mental processes. She was hiding, and she knew it. It worked, though. She managed to get by just fine. She was her own boss and could do what she wanted. Yeah, sometimes she had a hard time making decisions about big things, but for the most part, she was fine.

Beth climbed the stairs and walked into the bathroom before she realized that Mason was following her. She turned around and glared at him.

"I didn't invite you."

"I'm going to take a shower. I won't bother you. I've been up since five this morning. I need a shower." He started undressing.

Without giving him a second look, she turned her back and started the water in the tub. She waited until he was in the shower before she undressed and slipped into the water. She hoped he had cold water for his shower. It would serve him right. He could have taken one in the bathroom down the hall. She quickly bathed in hopes of finishing before he did, but about the time she stood up to get out of the tub, he was stepping out of the shower. They stared at each other.

"Get dried off, baby, before you catch cold." He sighed and grabbed a towel.

He turned his back to her as he dried off. She realized he was trying to give her some privacy. It went against everything she'd been building up about him being manipulative and demanding. How could she hold a grudge when he did something like that? Maybe he had just needed a shower.

Maybe she was reading into it all too much. They might just want a fling, and she was putting forever into it and balking at the idea of living a D/s lifestyle. There were plenty of them in Riverbend. She knew they were into that. And she wasn't anymore. They would want someone to live the life twenty-four-seven. She wasn't that woman. She'd never wanted to do that. It was one of the things she'd had a problem with Master James and Master Williams's offer. She just didn't want that sort of life.

Once she had her clothes back on, Mason walked out of the bathroom with his lower body wrapped in a towel. It didn't hide the obvious erection that tented the towel. She quickly averted her eyes, but not before Mason smiled at her. Then he turned away and walked down the hall toward his bedroom.

Beth hurried downstairs to the relative safety of her computer. There she could do anything she wanted and be anyone she wanted to be. It was never permanent, and there was always a "happy ever after" in it.

Mason passed the dining room and disappeared into the kitchen. She heard his voice a few minutes later. *He must be talking on the phone. I bet he's talking to Mac. He's probably telling him about the call. I hope he's calm by the time he gets here. I don't need another hassle today. I've had plenty.*

The sound of the cabinets opening and closing without further phone noises signaled that he had hung up. She relaxed for just a few minutes before digging in and surging forward with her writing. As much as she wanted to finish the book, she also wanted to make sure that it stayed true to how she wrote. With everything going on, she was worried that it would affect her voice.

She wasn't sure how long she had been writing when the security panel beeped and the back door opened. She heard Mason greet Mac and braced herself for whatever he might say or do. When he didn't immediately come looking for her, she frowned. What was going on? She refused to let her curiosity get the best of her. Instead she buried her head in her book and nearly screamed when he walked up behind her.

"You scared me to death."

"You get entirely too wrapped up in writing. I could have been the fucking stalker, and you wouldn't have known I was there."

"You said I was safe here. Either I am or I'm not, Mac. Which is it?" She was angry now. He'd scared her and then fussed at her.

"Mac." Mason walked in and looked at him.

Mac stood up and drew in a deep breath before letting it slowly out.

"Mason said the stalker called again."

"Yes. He's looking for me, Mac. What happens when he finds me?" She hugged herself as if a draft had blown by her.

"Nothing is going to happen to you. We're going to catch this bastard. Now that we know Larry is out, we have someone to look for. I've gotten his picture and have a copy all over town now. Everyone is looking for him. He won't be able to stay hidden for long." Mac ran a hand across the back of his neck.

"What if it's not him?"

"It has to be him, Beth. He got out about the same time you started having trouble."

"How did he find out about my writing? I wasn't writing when I was there."

"You were editing, right?"

"Yes, but I'd never really talked about writing. Well. Not really. I fussed about the authors I read not really knowing what they were talking about."

"He could have put two and two together by something that was in a book you wrote." Mac put two fingers beneath her chin and lifted it. "We'll find him, Beth, and we'll put him away for a long time."

She nodded but didn't feel as confident as Mac sounded. She knew from experience that sometimes things didn't work out like you planned.

* * * *

Mac hated seeing her look so discouraged, but there was nothing he could do. He wanted her alert, and as long as she was writing, she would lose her focus on anything but the book. If she wasn't writing, she was a nervous wreck. She wouldn't be any good in that state either. All he could do was hope that they caught Larry before he found her.

He left her sitting at the dining room table and headed for the bathroom. He wanted a shower before cooking. Mason was there if she needed anything. Right now, all he could think about was taking her to bed. His cock was rock hard, but he wouldn't risk the time it would take to jack off. He didn't want to be away from her even that long. If he had his way, she would be plastered to either his or Mason's side at all times.

As soon as he had dried off, Mac put on jeans and a T-shirt. He bounded down the stairs and checked on her before settling in to cook. Mason was reading over his case notes in the room with her. Satisfied that she was being watched, he decided on grilled chicken breasts with sautéed vegetables on a bed of rice.

He had everything ready within an hour. When he called them in to eat, neither one of them heard him. He stomped into the dining room. They both looked up with confused expressions on their faces.

"Did neither one of you hear me call you in to eat?"

"Sorry, Mac." Beth scooted her chair back and stood up. Mason did the same but looked worried.

Beth hurried into the kitchen. Mac waited to see what Mason had to say.

"I'm not worth crap until this fucking trial is over with. No need to be watching her instead of me." He was disgusted, and Mac understood that.

"Neither one of us has much of a choice right now. I have to work just like you do. She's safe here. We have to believe that and find the bastard."

"I hope you can find him soon. I'm getting worried. The longer he's out there, the less chance we have, Mac. You know that."

"Come on. Let's eat. I want to hold Beth for a while."

"Good luck with that. She's trying her best to keep her distance."

"We'll see."

They walked back into the kitchen and settled down to eat. Each of them was wrapped up in their own thoughts. Mac watched Beth eat, noting that she didn't seem to have much of an appetite. He wanted to tell her to eat more, but he decided to pick his battles and right now, she was eating enough to survive. They could fuss over her eating habits later.

Once they had finished, Mason was left with the dishes, and Mac led Beth into the living room where he settled her on the couch next to him.

"I need to be writing, Mac. I have a deadline."

"And you are ahead of deadline according to what you told your agent."

"It doesn't mean I'm going to stay ahead. I'm not writing at my best right now. I'm going to fall behind if I'm not careful."

"A few hours aren't going to hurt you that much, Beth. Let me hold you for a little while."

"Why?" She truly looked confused by his request.

"Because I care about you, and I'm worried about you. I need to hold you so that I know you are safe."

She shrugged but didn't press him or try and pull away when he pulled her closer. After a few minutes, she relaxed against him. He sighed. Finally, she seemed a little more comfortable around him. He pressed his luck and lowered his head to kiss her. He moved slowly so as not to startle her and to give her ample opportunity to pull away should she really want to.

When she didn't, he drew closer until his lips were a hair's breath away from hers. He closed the distance and sipped from hers before drawing in the lower one to lick and nip. Then he thrust his tongue inside her mouth in imitation of fucking her. She whimpered and began to kiss him back. Triumph fueled him on. They dueled for several seconds before he pulled away and rained kisses all along the corners of her mouth and around her jaw to her neck. He sucked in her earlobe, nipping it with his teeth then soothing it with his tongue. When he returned to her neck, he licked and kissed his way down to her shoulder.

She shivered as he nudged aside the collar of her shirt and bit her shoulder. Beth threw her head back and moaned. Mason walked up behind her and helped him lift her shirt over her head. Mac licked along the tops of her breasts as Mason unfastened her bra. Once they had it off of her, she seemed to come to herself and started to cover herself.

"No, baby. We want to make love to you. Let us love you, Beth. We'll take good care of you."

"You want more from me than I have to give, Mac. I can't be who you want me to be," she said on a light sob.

"How do you know what we want until we tell you? You're exactly what we want, baby. You're perfect for us whether you realize it or not."

Mac stood up then leaned over and scooped her up into his arms to carry her upstairs. She didn't protest or struggle. Mason followed them up, removing his clothes as they entered the bedroom. He took her from Mac so that he could undress as well. Then they both finished removing Beth's clothes.

Mac stared down into her heavy-lidded eyes and knew she was just as aroused as they were. When they pulled off her underwear, she was soaking wet. He could smell her now and wanted between her legs, but Mason hadn't gotten a taste of her yet. It was his turn. Mac would love on her breasts. They were magnificent breasts, too.

He ran his tongue all around a nipple while playing with the other one using his fingers. She arched her back into his hand and mouth. She responded so well to their touch. When Mason began kissing and sucking on her pussy lips, she moaned and rocked her pelvis toward his mouth.

"She tastes like ambrosia, Mac. I could lick her sweet pussy for hours."

"I told you. She creams with just a little stimulation. Wait until she clamps down on your fingers. You'll want to come with her."

Mac watched as Mason consumed Beth's pussy, and then he returned to tormenting her breasts with his mouth and hands. He wanted inside her cunt so badly it hurt. There had to be a way to convince her they were the ones for her.

Chapter Eleven

Everything was closing in on her. Mason had his fingers inside her cunt, pumping them lightly as he sucked on her pussy. Mac continued to suck on her nipples one at a time until she felt as if she would come undone just by his mouth there. A barrage of emotions flooded her mind as their stimulations flooded her body with pleasure.

Mason curled his fingers inside of her, locating her hot spot and attacking it as if with one goal in mind. She felt her pleasure building with each swipe of his fingers and each draw of Mac's mouth on her breasts.

It would be devastating when it happened. She was convinced it would kill her as massive as it seemed to be. She fought it at first, and then she realized it was useless. They were going to wring it out of her one way or another. She finally gave in and let it roll over her and through her. She screamed as her cunt contracted around Mason's fingers. He cursed and sucked in her clit, which sent her soaring even higher.

"She's fucking breaking my fingers."

"Told you. She's like a dam that suddenly breaks and washes everything away."

Mac's voice sent shivers down her body even as she slowly sank back to earth. She was dimly aware of Mason crawling up her body and licking his way across her chest as Mac stroked her face.

"You okay, baby?"

"I'll never be the same again," she managed to whisper.

"I want inside that tight cunt, Beth. Will you let me make you feel good?"

"Oh, God. You're going to kill me, Mac. I can't keep doing this. I'll lose myself."

"No, baby. You'll find yourself."

He tore a condom open and rolled it over his massive erection. Then he positioned himself between her legs and pushed into her tight pussy. She thrashed on the bed as he began to thrust over and over in an effort to lodge himself as deep as possible inside her tight cunt.

Mason whispered how pretty she was, and how he couldn't wait to get inside her. She couldn't help but thrust her pelvis up to meet Mac's relentless pumping in and out of her. When he pushed his hands beneath her ass and held her up, he surged deeper and bumped her cervix. The pleasure-pain did it for her. She couldn't stop the scream when it burst from her mouth. She went wild as he bumped her over and over again.

His cock pummeled her pussy even as she attempted to dig her way through the mattress with her fingers. Mason licked and nipped at her breasts, pulling on them and twisting them to add to her pleasure.

"Please, I need to come, Mac. Do something." She begged for him to make her come. She didn't care how it sounded.

He pressed her clit between them, and she bowed her back even as he thrust inside of her.

"Fuck! That's it, baby. Squeeze my dick." He moved inside her twice more then stilled as he came.

Beth's ears were roaring as she tried to catch her breath. Then Mac was moving aside and Mason licked her thighs inside and all over her pelvis as he took his place. She couldn't imagine coming again, but Mason wanted his turn. She couldn't deny them anything even if she wanted to. She was totally hooked on their loving.

Mason coaxed her to roll over to her hands and knees. Mac helped her steady herself, and Mason's sheathed cock pushed against her swollen slit. He slid into her pussy until he finally made it halfway inside of her. He grunted and pulled out only to surge back inside and lodge himself balls deep inside her cunt.

"God, she is so fucking tight. My cock is never going to be the same again."

Beth didn't think she would ever be the same again, either, as he pulled out and pushed back in, over and over. He slowly built speed as his thick dick stretched her pussy wide. It was almost painful. He was so large.

"Aw, hell. Squeeze me again, baby."

She squeezed her cunt down around his swollen cock and as he pumped in and out of her. She slowly began to meet him thrust for thrust as she threw her head back intent on the pleasure trying to sneak up on her. She would never have thought she could climax again, but it built as Mason tunneled in and out of her cunt.

"I'm fucking not going to last."

Mac pulled and tugged on her nipples. He whispered in her ear.

"Play with your clit, baby. Show us how you like it. Make yourself come."

She looked up at him, uncertainty filling her with worry. The Masters hadn't liked for her to play with herself, often forbidding her to come when she was alone.

"Do it, Beth. Play with yourself."

She reached between her legs and ran her finger back to her slit where she could feel Mason's cock stretching her swollen pussy. Then she slid back and located her clit with her fingers. Beth began to press and circle her clit, over and over until she exploded in intense pleasure. She cried out Mason's name, unable to keep from doing it.

A few seconds later as she slowly drifted down, Mason stilled behind her with his cock shoved deep in her cunt. His shout of release sent a thrill through her that he'd come just seconds behind her.

Beth was unable to continue to hold herself up. When Mason collapsed on top of her, she went down with the pressure. He chuckled. It was an odd feeling with him buried deep inside her.

"What's so funny?" She frowned, trying to wiggle from beneath him.

"I came so hard that I lost the feeling in my fingers and toes for a few seconds. You're deadly, Beth."

"Get off of her, Mason. She can't breathe." Mac punched him lightly in the arm.

"Sorry, baby." He rolled off of her and headed toward the bathroom.

Beth buried her head in the covers. She couldn't believe she'd just had sex with them. What had she been thinking? She hadn't. That was the entire problem. She couldn't think around them. She needed the security people to finish with her house so she could put some distance between them. After this, she wouldn't be able to say no to them.

"What's going through that busy head of yours, baby?" Mac asked.

"That you're bad for me. Very bad. I need to go home, Mac. I need to get back into my routine. I don't like living like this."

"Like what, Beth?" Mac had grown still.

"Like not knowing what is going on and having no schedule. I like my schedule, Mac."

"Then set up a schedule here, because you aren't going back until we catch this guy. He's too smart, Beth."

She flung the covers back and started to get up. Mason walked back in and stopped her from getting out of the bed.

"Where are you going, baby? It's time to go to bed." He scooted in next to her, and then wrapped his arm around her waist.

"You're both just alike. I don't care if you're not identical twins. You're manipulative and bossy."

"You're reckless and in need of a keeper, baby," Mason said. "You don't eat regularly, and you forget what time it is."

"I've been doing just fine without the two of you interfering in my life. I will be fine once you're gone."

Mac growled and pulled her out of Mason's embrace into his arms. He covered her mouth with his, devouring hers as he pulled her even closer to him. He kissed her with his teeth and tongue until she was sure she would die from lack of oxygen. Then he released her and stared down at her.

"Tell me you're not soaking wet right now. Fucking tell me that you're not so hot that you would rub on my leg if nothing else." He was breathing just as hard as she was.

She glared at him because he was right. She was hot and wet enough to boil an egg. His mastering her did it for her. It turned her inside out, and she knew nothing would ever compete with the way Mason and Mac fucked her.

"It's just sex, Mac. It doesn't mean anything." Even as she said it, Beth knew it was a lie. It meant a great deal to her.

"No, Beth. We made love to you. You can't belittle what we have by calling it sex." Mason jerked her attention to him. "I won't let you."

"Whether you like it or not, you're ours now. You belong to us. We'll take good care of you and provide you with everything you need, but you're ours, Beth." Mac's words sent her heart reeling in her chest.

"Please, Mac, Mason. Let me go. I can't be what you want, what you need."

"How do you know, Beth, when you don't know what we need? What makes you think you know when we haven't told you?"

"You're looking for a submissive to live with you, someone who will live the life and allow you to control everything in her life. I can't do that. I have my own thoughts and needs."

"Have we asked you to give up anything? And we're not looking for a pet, Beth. We want a wife."

She gasped and scrambled out of his arms toward the foot of the bed. That had taken her totally by surprise. She hadn't expected that they not only wanted something permanent, but legally permanent as well. She sat there for what felt like a full minute just staring at the two men.

"Why me? You've known me for years, and never once since I've been back have you approached me. Why?"

"We didn't think you would be able to handle our lifestyle. You'd run before. We thought you might run again."

"What changed your mind? It couldn't have been this stalker I've picked up."

"In a manner of speaking, it was. We found out you had experience in the D/s relationship and even wrote about it. You were the one we secretly wanted for years now. To suddenly find out that you're attainable has taken away some of our good sense. We've gone about this all wrong. We should have wooed you and taken you out before we got so deep into it. Unfortunately, the stalker put a rush on things. Having you here only made us want you more and we couldn't keep our hands off of you." Mac ran a hand through his hair before reaching for her.

Beth leaned back to avoid his hand. If he touched her, she would surely give in to them. She needed to be strong and stand up for herself. She needed to go home. But if Mason and Mac had their way, she wouldn't be going there anytime soon. She was too scared to stay at home alone without a good security system now, and she doubted they were going to let one be installed anytime soon.

A cold lethargy stole over her as she realized she was effectively trapped for now. She would have to live by their rules until they had caught the stalker. Then she would return to her house and her rules. They could go jump in a lake.

She let out a long breath before slowly climbing back beneath the covers and lying down on her back. She stared up at the ceiling and willed her heart to slow down. She felt as if it would race right out of her chest.

"Beth, baby. Give us a chance. That's all we're asking. Not right now, but after all of this is over with." Mason ran a finger across her face to move her hair out of her eyes. "Say you'll at least think about it, baby."

"I don't know. I already know it won't work. Why put ourselves through it in the first place?"

"Because I think it will, because I think you're worth it." Mason continued stroking her cheek.

Mac drew in a deep breath and let it out. Beth could tell that he was still upset with her for doubting them. A part of her wanted to apologize and tell them that they were right and she was wrong, but if she did that, she would be lost. Another part of her told her she was crazy for turning them down without giving a relationship with them a chance. The sane part of her said it was all wishful thinking, and that she needed to get as far away from them as possible before it was too late.

"Go to sleep, Beth. We'll talk about it in the morning."

Mac's tired voice made her wince. She knew that having her there was disrupting their lives. It was all the more reason that she needed to go back home. They would need to have a conversation about that this weekend. If they weren't working on her house by then, she would hire someone else to install the damn security system.

She wasn't going to push them until then. Mason had his trial going on, and Mac was trying to catch her stalker. She owed them for helping her when she was being less than cooperative. Still, they were demanding more than just following their orders. They wanted her to change her life. As much as she cared about them and wanted them, Beth had to resist their pull.

She lay awake a long time after the two of them had fallen asleep. She couldn't get something out of her mind. Why had the stalker said that he always knew what she needed? It was as if he had known her for a long time. Larry had known her for a long time, and he was out there somewhere. Was he really her stalker? How had he found out about her writing?

She hadn't started writing until well over a year later. Very few people actually knew about her writing and out of that handful, only her agent and her publisher knew who she wrote as. The more she thought about it, the more she thought that it wasn't Larry.

He wouldn't have been able to do any research on her while he was in the hospital, would he? He'd been out about a month, so he would have had to work fast to find out all her secrets. If not Larry, then who? Who else knew about her?

Mason and Mac had the resources to have done everything, plant bugs and cameras in her house, find out about her writing. They would have known that they could convince her to move in with them if it seemed that she was in danger. But Mason had been there at the house when the stalker had called earlier that day. What about Mac?

Beth wasn't sure what to think anymore. Maybe she should go to Dallas and stay with the Masters. Somehow that didn't hold much appeal to her. Leaving Mac and Mason didn't hold much appeal either, but she needed to put some distance between them.

Finally, she settled her mind down enough that she was able to relax. She couldn't help snuggling closer to Mac's back as she fell asleep. Her last thought was that if they were her stalkers, then she wasn't really in any danger at all.

Chapter Twelve

Mason was gone the next morning when she woke up. Mac was in the shower from the sound of the water running in the bathroom. She stretched and found that she was slightly sore in key places. She felt heat rush to her face at the wanton way she'd behaved the night before. She had no excuse other than they had seduced her and she obviously was easily seduced, by them, at least.

Beth pulled on her clothes and padded down the hall to the other bathroom, and then she hurried downstairs to make coffee. She called herself seven kinds of a fool for wanting to have it ready when he came down. It was another indication that she needed to leave. She already wanted to please them.

"I smell coffee. Thanks, Beth. I'm running late." Mac walked in wearing his uniform and looking dangerous.

"When are they going to be finished with my security system?"

Mac paused with his cup halfway to his mouth. "You'll have to ask Mason to check for you. He knows the guys doing it."

"Okay. I guess if they aren't working on it soon, I'll just find someone else."

Mac didn't say anything, but she could see the wheels in his mind turning. She figured he was trying to think of a way to stall her.

"I'm going to be in the office most of the day if you need me. I called in a part-time deputy to take some of the load off of the rest of us."

"Okay, I doubt I'll need anything. All I'm going to be doing is writing. Don't worry about lunch. I'll fix a sandwich here." She sipped her coffee and waited to see what he'd come up with.

"That might be a good idea. I need to catch up on paperwork in case we get busy. Remember, don't answer the door and don't answer the phone unless it's someone you know."

"I won't. Don't you think it's going to make the stalker mad if he can't reach me to terrorize me?"

Mac set his coffee cup down and scowled at her. "You're not taking this very seriously anymore. The man is dangerous, Beth. Don't screw around and think that he's not."

"I'm not, Mac. I'm just frustrated. What's going to happen when he can't reach me?"

"I'm hoping it will make him angry enough that he'll make a mistake. When he does that, we catch him."

"I hope you're right, Mac." She climbed off the barstool where she had perched and took her coffee into the dining room to start writing.

A few minutes later, Mac walked in. She had been reading over what she had done the night before to get back into her groove. She looked up to see what he wanted. When he only stood there looking at her, she squirmed.

"What is it?"

"Nothing. I'm just looking at you. I can't get enough of you, Beth. Every time I stop doing something, you wiggle your way into my thoughts. I don't want to lose you."

"You can't lose something you never had in the first place, Mac. I've never been yours or Mason's."

"You've been ours since that day in the park all those years ago." With that, he turned around and walked out of the room. A few seconds later, she heard the security system beep, and then the door to the garage opened and closed.

Beth found herself staring into space several minutes later, her mind seemingly a total blank. She shook it off and jumped into her writing. She could find so much in her stories. They helped her relieve stress and frustration. But today, they could do nothing at helping her to get past Mason and Mac's loving from the night before.

She found herself reliving every gasp, purr, and sigh over and over. She even found that she'd incorporated parts of it into her own love scene. She started to erase the entire chapter and start over, but something made her leave it. This book would be her reminder of the time she spent with them once she was home again and everything was back to normal.

I'm crazy for wanting them in the first place. Never mind that I know how good it could be. I can't allow them to sway me. It would be a disaster.

Shaking her head, Beth finally managed to put it all out of her head and concentrate on writing. Hours later, her stomach growled, letting her know that it was time to eat. She hadn't eaten anything for breakfast. She still had a half of a cup of cold coffee sitting on the table now.

With a groan, she stood up and stretched. Then she carried the forgotten coffee and poured it out in the sink. She dug around in the refrigerator until she found sandwich meat and located a loaf of bread in the pantry. After making one for herself, she replaced everything and sat down at the bar to eat. She had poured a glass of tea and noticed the pitcher was almost empty, so she fixed a boiler of tea and left it to sit while she ate.

Later, she returned to the dining room and her computer to concentrate on a particularly difficult scene. She had been writing on it before lunch, but she still wasn't pleased with it. She lost herself in her work once again when her phone rang. She picked it up only to discover that it was a long distance number. She started to answer it anyway, but she had promised not to. She waited until the ringing stopped, and then she put in a call to Mac.

"Hey, Beth. What is it?"

"I think he called back. It was an unlisted phone number. I didn't answer it. It looks like he left a voice mail. Should I listen to it?"

"No! I'll be home in a few minutes and see what it says. Just stay where you are and…"

"Don't answer the door. I know, Mac."

After he'd disconnected, Beth sat there staring at the phone. She could listen to it, and he would never know. Only somehow, he would know. Something in her eyes or on her face would tip him off. She sighed and resigned herself to waiting until he managed to make it home.

Oddly enough, she didn't have long to wait. She heard the crunch of tires as a car pulled up outside the dining room windows. She refrained from peeking through the blinds. Mac would have something to say about that, too. She waited until she heard the beep, beep of the alarm and the closing snap of the back door.

A few seconds later, Mac walked in with a strained expression marring his handsome face.

"Larry hasn't been seen or heard from since his discharge. He isn't required to check in with anyone, either. He will need his medication refilled sometime in the next month or so. He had a three-month supply."

"Great. So we don't know if he's in this area or not. We're just guessing."

"It's got to be him, Beth. It makes sense."

"I still don't see how he found out what I was doing from the hospital or in the space of a week before he showed up as my Peeping Tom. Neither can I figure out how he found out my pseudonym. The name isn't from anyone I know or anyone I even talked about. I completely made it up. I stuck with it because I liked the way it sounded."

"Until we get something else to go on, it's all we have." He picked up her phone and pushed some buttons.

The mechanical voice spoke out from the speaker of the speaker phone.

"I'm disappointed in you, Beth. I thought you had more respect for yourself than to take up with the Tidwells. They have a reputation for using women then kicking them to the side. Did you know that, Beth? You're much better off with me. I'll give you everything you need. I'm coming for you, Beth, darling." Then he cut off.

She drew in a shaky breath as his words sank in. He now knew that she was staying with them. He didn't know for sure if anything had actually happened between them, though. She wasn't sure if that was to their advantage or not.

"What is he going to do next?" she asked with a shaky voice.

"I don't know, but he's not happy you're staying with us. I think we can up the stress level for him and get him to screw up so we can catch him sooner."

"How do we do that?" Beth wasn't sure she was going to like this.

"We go out in public together. He sees us cozying up to you, and he just might make a move sooner."

"I'm game for anything to flush him out. I'm tired of this living like a hermit. I never went out much, but if I wanted ice cream at midnight, I could run up to the grocery store and buy a half-pint and not worry about it."

"I know, baby. You miss your independence. It won't be much longer."

I need to write this down. I'll go to the kitchen and copy it off the phone so you don't have to hear it played out over and over.

"Thanks. The mechanical voice is just plain creepy."

Mac took the phone and disappeared into the kitchen. A few minutes later, Beth was once again deep inside her book when Mac walked back in. She looked up then returned her attention back to the computer keyboard and screen. The love scene was almost finished now. She needed another two hundred words to round it out.

"Beth, he knows who you are, and now he knows where you are. We've never been friendly before, so it wasn't a logical leap. Think, Beth. Who have you told where you are?"

"No one. I haven't told anyone where I am." She felt like she was forgetting something.

"My agent knows I'm in Riverbend, but she doesn't know where I'm staying right now. Neither does my publisher."

"Okay. We'll go with the assumption that he put two and two together when you weren't at your house anymore. He could find out that we've brought in food here lately, enough for three."

"How are we going to be seen together?"

"I figure we'll go out to eat and then maybe go dancing for an hour or so. That will give us plenty of exposure. He won't try to make a move in public, so you'll be safe with us." Mac walked around behind her chair and rested his hands on her shoulders.

Beth wasn't sure what to do. Heat from his hands seeped into her skin, making her shiver.

"Mac?"

"Beth."

"What are you doing?"

"Touching you."

He began to massage her there then rubbed his thumbs against the base of her neck. When he moved back to her shoulders, he spread his fingers out until he was touching just about every place he could at one time.

"You're so tense, baby. Why don't you let me give you a massage and help you relax?"

"Hmm. I don't think that's a good idea. I'll get sleepy, and then I won't write. I need to be writing, Mac."

He seemed to increase the pressure in his hands, and soon she was moaning and had laid her head on the table. She couldn't believe how good it felt. Much more and she would take a nap. Maybe a nap wasn't such a bad idea.

"I think I'll take a nap on the couch."

"Sounds like a very good idea. Come on. I'll help you relax and massage you until you fall asleep."

She stumbled when she started to walk into the other room. Mac swooped her into his arms and carried her to the couch. Then he gently stood her on her feet.

"Let's get you comfortable for your nap." He pulled off her shirt before she knew what he was going to do.

"Hey! What are you doing?"

"Getting you comfortable. You'll sleep better without clothes on."

She looked into his eyes and saw nothing but concern there. She helped him remove her shoes and then her jeans. She stretched out on the couch so that Mac could get to her. He straddled her hips and began kneading her muscles in her neck, shoulders, and back. Then he did her upper arms.

"Mmm, so good." She was just about asleep.

He moved lower and manipulated her lower back and then her buttocks. She stiffened at first when he touched the bare cheeks of her ass, but then relaxed again. All he did was rub her skin to relax her. Finally, he stood up and pulled an afghan over her. He knelt by her head for a few minutes and smoothed her hair from her face. Then he kissed her gently on the cheek and walked away.

Beth couldn't believe he was leaving after getting her to the point that she would have done just about anything for him. Maybe they had gotten the message that she wasn't interested. Only she was interested, very interested, but she knew they were more than she could handle. With that last thought, she drifted off to sleep.

* * * *

Mac slammed the phone down on the desk. No one had seen Larry anywhere. He hadn't shown up at any of his old hangouts, according to Mac's friends in Dallas. Neither had anyone noticed him around Riverbend. Where could the guy be hiding?

He checked his watch and found that it was about time to head home. Mason's trial had taken an early recess, and he was supposed to be home by six. They had talked and were going to take Beth out to eat. They had decided to wait until the weekend to go dancing. Mason had one more day left that week for the trial, and he needed to be at his best.

Connie walked into his office with a pile of paperwork. He groaned but nodded when she started to walk back out.

"Come on in, Connie. What do you need?"

"I have the reports from yesterday ready. Do you want to look at them now or in the morning?"

"Anything interesting or unusual that I might need to look at tonight?"

"Well, Mrs. Caskill says there are aliens camping out in the woods behind her house. The Jameses are fighting again, and Jared and Quade reported a stolen cow."

"Mrs. Caskill has aliens on the brain. Last month they were filming her house from the trees across the street. Any bloodshed on the Jameses?"

"No. Mostly name-calling."

"Who's handling the cow? Jared and Quade don't usual report something like a lost cow."

"Isn't lost. Someone broke into their barn and stole the cow. They were keeping it there because it had a bad cut on its shoulder, and Silas is working on that one."

"Okay, I'll read the rest tomorrow when I come in. Thanks, Connie. Just leave them on my desk."

Connie stacked the papers in a neat pile in the center of his desk and walked out with her head down. She rarely smiled or talked unless spoken to. He wished he knew why she was so quiet, but he wasn't going to push her.

Once again, he started for the door and managed to get through it this time without another setback. He said good-night to Jace, one of his other deputies, and headed for his truck. If he hurried, he would get there about the same time as Mason was due home.

He wondered how long Beth had slept after he'd left her on the couch. It had been hard as hell to walk away without riding her until they were both worn out. He knew that she would have welcomed his attentions by the way she had responded to his hands on her body, but he needed to prove to her that it wasn't all about the sex. It was a big part of it, but not all of it and certainly not the most important piece by far.

He and Mason wanted her as their wife and partner. They wanted to share with her all the joys of a ménage relationship, but she had to want it, too. He wasn't sure why she was balking, but it had to do with their statuses as Masters, he was sure. He could easily understand why she didn't trust easily when it came to the BDSM lifestyle. But she could trust them. He had to somehow prove to her that she could.

Trust was something that had to be earned, and when she wouldn't even let them approach her, there wasn't much chance of earning anything. So, he was starting from square one. He hoped he had passed the first test when he'd walked away that afternoon. He would see how she reacted around them tonight.

He pulled into the drive and parked behind Mason's truck. When he got inside, it was to find Mason standing in the kitchen with a beer in one hand and his cell phone in the other. He nodded at Mac as he walked by. It sounded like he was talking to someone about the case. He thought he would find Beth in the dining room, but she wasn't there. He needed to change out of his uniform and shower. Maybe she was upstairs. He'd check on his way to his room.

When he knocked on the master bedroom door and walked in, it was to find Beth dressed in a pair of navy blue slacks and a pretty red sweater. He was sure it had some special name for the shade, but it was red to him. Either way, it made her look really nice.

"Hey, baby. How are you feeling?"

"Does this look okay? I don't go out much to know how I need to dress."

"You look fine. I like that sweater on you."

She smiled so that her eyes shone. "Thanks."

"I'm going to shower and change clothes. I'll be downstairs in about thirty minutes, and we'll go."

"Okay. I'll keep Mason company. I have a feeling the trial isn't going as well as he thought it would. He was uptight when he got here."

"Uh-oh. Thanks for the warning." He quickly dropped a kiss on her cheek before she realized what he was going to do. Then he headed toward his room.

If the trial wasn't going well and that bastard got off, he wasn't sure what they would do. David Reeves has swindled several of the older people in town out of quite a bit of money. It had taken quite a bit of work to locate him and then bring him in for trial. The man was as slick as a greased pig and smelled just as bad.

He hoped Mason would be able to put it behind him for a couple of hours and be on guard. They needed to concentrate on keeping Beth safe and watching for anything unusual around them. He prayed he wasn't making a mistake putting her out in the spotlight. He would never get over it if something happened to her.

Chapter Thirteen

They walked into the Riverbend Fish and Steak house at a quarter to eight. The place was busy for a Thursday night. Beth had been there a few times, but not often. It wasn't that it was outside her price range, but she just didn't go places much. No doubt Mac and Mason had been there often.

The waitress seated them at a table in the back where it was a little quieter than up front where most of the larger families were seated. She had to smile at one family with three children. The kids were fairly well behaved, but the parents were still busy with them. It was a good thing there were two fathers.

"What are you smiling at, Beth?" Mason asked.

"That family over there." She nodded toward the one she was talking about. "The parents are having a good time keeping up with their kids."

The waitress took their drink orders and hurried off to fill them. Beth wasn't sure what they were supposed to do. She knew they were putting her out there some to stir up the stalker's anger, so he would make a mistake, but how exactly did they plan to do that eating out?

"How was your day, Beth?" Mac asked.

"I got a good bit accomplished on my book. It's moving along on schedule. What about you? Were you busy today?"

"No more than usual. Seems that there are aliens living out in the woods, someone stole a cow, and the normal squabbles between people. Nothing exciting to report." He turned toward Mason. "What about you? How is the trial going?"

"What little I can say about it is that it's not as cut-and-dried as we had hoped."

"I'm sorry, Mason. You've been working so hard on it. Do you think you'll be able to prove your case?" Beth could see the worry in Mason's eyes.

"I'm confident everything will be fine, just not as confident as I was the first part of the week."

The waitress returned with their drinks, and they ordered their food. Beth chose fried catfish and hush puppies. Both Mason and Mac ordered steaks, medium rare. Once the waitress had left again, Mac leaned forward.

"Beth, I want you to act real friendly toward us. We want to make him jealous and angry that we've got you and he doesn't."

"What do I do?"

"Hold our hands, let us kiss you."

"Are you sure this is for his benefit?" she asked, suspicious now of their real motives.

"Beth, you know where we stand. We want you. But this is about catching the guy stalking you and not about our feelings toward you." Mason reached out and brushed his finger down her cheek.

Beth couldn't help but turn her face into the light caress. He smiled at her and lengthened the touch. The expression on his face sent her juices spilling. It wouldn't be long before her panties would be soaked. She hoped she didn't leave a wet spot on the chair. Her pussy reacted to both men like a puppy followed his owner.

Throughout the evening, the men took every opportunity to touch her. They brushed kisses along the backs of her hands and at her cheek. Mac would hold her hand for a while, and then Mason would take over. She didn't have to pretend to enjoy herself. She truly did. They were attentive men who appeared to dote on their date. What she wouldn't give to be able to bask in the warmth of their love.

But they hadn't professed love, and she wasn't in the market for a new Master or Masters as the case may be. She couldn't live that life again. It was too risky. She no longer took risks except in her books. There she could do and be anyone or anything she wanted. No one got hurt, and everyone lived happily ever after.

"Are you ready to go now?" Mac was asking her.

"I'm ready whenever you guys are."

Mason and Mac stood and helped her from her chair. Mason took her elbow and guided her through the restaurant with Mac forging the way. They stopped at several tables to chat on the way out. She knew a good many of the patrons that night, but not as many as Mac and Mason knew. She was introduced as their girlfriend. She hadn't thought about how they would handle that. She supposed it was the right thing to do since they were trying to make her stalker mad.

Once out in the parking lot, Mason wrapped his arm around her and pulled her in close to his body. Mac walked on the other side and crowded them as they headed for the truck. She was totally unprepared when Mason swung her around so that her back was to Mac. Then he closed the short distance between them and drew her into a kiss.

Beth relaxed in his arms and let him kiss her. It was all for show, she assured herself. She even wrapped her arms around his neck. When she felt Mac grinding his hard cock against the small of her back, she pressed back into it and rubbed. Mac growled in her ear. But it was all for show. It didn't mean anything.

When Mason lifted his head from her mouth, his eyes were heavy lidded, and arousal tented his dress slacks.

"Just wait until we get you back to the house, baby. We're going to take good care of you." Mason's husky voice was a little louder than was necessary, but she knew he wanted his words to carry.

Mac nipped at her neck and whispered in her ear. "Easy, baby. Everything is fine."

"I think we need to go now." Beth didn't like standing out in the open with them loving on her. She felt vulnerable, but she also felt a little trashy with other people hearing that she was about to go home with the two men and have sex. She hadn't thought that far ahead. Obviously neither had they.

Mason helped her up into the truck before climbing in next to her. Mac got in on the driver's side. They pulled out of the parking lot and headed directly to their house. Mason kept her tucked in under his arm next to him. He kissed her cheek and nibbled at her neck as they drove toward their place. She noticed Mac kept looking in the rearview mirror. She wanted to ask if someone was following them but didn't. She wasn't sure if she wanted to know the truth or not. Right now, she could pretend that it was all for show and that Mac and Mason weren't really working at arousing her.

The minute they were safely inside behind closed doors and blinds, she let out a pent-up breath that she'd been holding since they'd left the house. She fully expected the men to pull back and talk about what they had seen or noticed while they'd been out. Instead, Mason pinned her to the wall in the kitchen by the fridge and attacked her mouth. She was so startled that she didn't put up a fight. By the time she realized what was going on, she was too far gone to back away.

"God, Beth. I want you so badly. I hurt. Let us love you." Mason licked a long line from her shoulder, where he'd pushed back her sweater, to her ear, where he sucked in the lobe to play with it.

"You're so fucking sexy, baby. I want to bury my cock in your hot cunt," Mac whispered in her other ear.

"God, you are driving me crazy." Beth didn't know what to do.

Her body was betraying her. She knew they could smell her arousal. She knew it was a bad idea to let them make love to her again, but she couldn't say no. She wanted them as much as they wanted her.

"Mason, let's take her upstairs. I want a comfortable bed under us." Mac didn't wait for the other man to agree or disagree. He picked her up from Mason's arms and carried her upstairs in a near run.

Once upstairs, he knelt one knee on the bed and gently laid her down. They both hovered over her as she looked up at them. She wasn't sure what they were doing until she felt their hands working her clothes from her body. Once she was totally nude, they began removing their clothes, stopping occasionally to kiss her or touch her.

Beth shivered as a warm mouth left her body open to the cooler air in the room. They licked and sucked, bit and soothed her body from her toes to her head and all parts in between. Her pussy leaked her juices as they stimulated her all over. She wasn't sure where they would strike next, until Mason settled between her legs and began licking her pussy in long, languid strokes.

Mac knelt on the bed next to her head and tapped her lips with his cock. She rolled her eyes to look up at him, and the intense arousal in his heavy-lidded eyes sent her own arousal through the roof. She opened her mouth and let him feed his dick into it.

"Suck my cock, baby. I want to feel your hot mouth on my cock."

He wound his hand in her hair and held on as she licked all around the cockhead before sucking at the bottom of it. He tugged on her hair as she nipped at the fragile ring of the corona. Then she took him to the back of her throat and swallowed around him. He hissed out a breath. When she sucked hard on his cock on the way back up, he ran his hand lightly over her cheek.

Mason kissed the insides of her thighs before returning to her pussy to suck on her pussy lips while he ran his fingers around her slit. He teased her with them so that she thought he would enter her but then didn't. When he finally pushed two fingers inside her cunt, she moaned around Mac's cock. The vibrations caused him to moan and tighten his hold on her hair.

"That feels fucking wonderful, baby. Growl for me. I want to feel that again."

Beth growled around him in her mouth as she ran her tongue up and down the stalk. He began to slowly pump his cock in and out of her mouth. He took long, easy strokes. She lightly raked her teeth on his dick as he pushed in and sucked hard against him when he pulled out. He slowly picked up the pace and plunged deeper in her mouth.

"Relax your throat and let me in, baby. You can do it."

She did as he said and he bumped the back of her throat. She swallowed around him.

"Fuck! Do that again, baby. That's it. Just like that." He groaned and dug his fingers in her scalp.

Beth squealed around his cock as Mason chose that moment to curl his fingers and begin stroking her sweet spot. It had her pumping her hips into his face. She couldn't control herself as he rubbed that little spot over and over until she was unable to hold in her scream of climax. He immediately sucked on her clit at the same time and she felt as if her insides were swirling in a blender. Everything tilted as she cried out.

Mac pumped his cock in and out of her mouth until he too was climaxing. He shot his cum down her throat. She swallowed compulsively. His shout of completion echoed the one in her head as she spiraled out of control.

Mason continued to lick her clit in slow laps as he pulled his fingers from her cunt. The slow letdown helped her focus on breathing once Mac had pulled free of her mouth. She looked down at where Mason was sucking on her fingers. It was so naughty looking that she moaned as another shock wave traveled from her clit to her womb.

Mason reached for a condom off the bedside table and then rolled it on. He captured her eyes with his stare and slowly fed his thick dick into her still-spasming pussy. She gasped as he pushed his way through her pussy. He was so big. Mac was longer with a slight curve, but Mason was just thick.

"You're so fucking tight, Beth. I can't wait to get all the way inside your hot cunt. You're going to squeeze me to death."

"Please, please hurry. I need more." She gasped as he pulled out and plunged back in, stretching her pussy to its limit.

Mac licked on her nipples as Mason began to thrust inside of her harder and faster. The strength of his strokes would have shoved her further up the bed was it not for Mac's arm holding her still. He grasped her nipple and pulled at it as he nipped at the other one.

Mason grunted as he pummeled her pussy with his cock. She could feel the burning that signaled her climax was building. The pleasure-pain of his dick stretching her only added to the need growing with every stroke of his cock. She didn't think she would ever live through another set of climaxes like the ones from the night before. They didn't give her a choice, though. They attacked her with pleasure and demanded she accept it.

Beth squeezed her cunt muscles around Mason's cock as tightly as she could in hopes of hurrying him along. Much more and she was going to die. She had no doubt that he would send her screaming into eternity.

"Aw, hell! Yeah, baby. Squeeze me just like that."

She clamped down on him until he was struggling to pull out and push back in. His quick strokes became hard plunges, and she realized she had only increased her own climax to the point of explosion. When he leaned down and nipped her belly while Mac was twisting her nipples, she flew. She never even felt it when Mason climaxed. All Beth felt was the intense pleasure that enveloped her in a cloud of euphoria. She struggled to breathe through the thickness of it.

Long minutes later, Mac and Mason were stroking her shoulders and arms talking to her. She finally became aware of them whispering in her ears how beautiful she looked. She wasn't sure how long she'd been floating, but Mason was not panting, so it had to have been awhile.

"How are you doing, baby?" Mason asked, brushing a quick kiss across her lips.

"I'm dead. I can prove it. Just give me a second to relearn how to breathe."

Mason chuckled and settled his hand over her abdomen. Mac kissed along her cheek before nipping at her chin.

"How about a quick shower, babe?" Mac turned over and got out of bed.

"I'm not sure I can stand up."

"Don't worry about it. We'll hold you up."

Mason rolled out of bed on the other side before turning around to pick her up. The three of them walked to the bathroom where Mac turned on the water and adjusted the temperature before walking into it. Mason followed, carrying her. She shivered at the soft pelting of the water against her skin.

Mason carefully helped her to slide down his body and stand up. He steadied her as Mac began to lather her up with the soap and a bath cloth. Then they turned her around, and Mason rinsed her off as Mac started on her other side. He spent an extended period of time on her breasts, kneading them and pushing them up until she called him on it. He grinned like a little boy caught with his hand in the cookie jar.

"No more playing. I'm ready for bed."

"You heard her, Mason. No more playing."

They grabbed her and pulled her under the water until she was completely wet from head to toe. Then Mason grabbed some shampoo and began to lather her hair with it. She tried to take over, but Mac held her arm still.

"Let him wash your hair. He likes to do it."

She stopped struggling and let them finish with her. She didn't have the strength left to struggle anyway.

Once she was thoroughly rinsed, they climbed out of the shower and dried her off. Mason took a comb and the hair dryer and dried her hair until it was a soft mass of curls and waves. She doubted she would be able to do anything with it in the morning, but he'd obviously enjoyed it. She let it go.

Mac carried her back to bed and tucked her in with a kiss. Mason climbed in on the other side of her and pulled her back into his arms. Then Mac pulled her arm over his side, and she drifted into sleep, wondering how she was ever going to manage to leave them once her house was ready.

Chapter Fourteen

Friday at lunchtime, Beth looked up to see an obviously worried Mason walk through the dining room door. One look told her that the trial wasn't going well.

"How about you sit down, and I'll fix you something to eat?" She stood up and headed for the kitchen, but he stopped her, pulling her in for a kiss.

She relaxed into him as he plundered her mouth with his tongue. He nipped at her lower lip then licked along the roof of her mouth before fucking her with his tongue. She moaned as he pulled back and drew her into his arms.

"Thanks, I needed a hug."

"How about lunch?"

"I'm really not so hungry. Do you feel like sitting on the couch for a while? Do you have time?"

"Sure."

She took his hand and led him to the couch. When he sat down, she acted on impulse and sank to her knees between his legs. His eyes widened in question until she unfastened his pants and pulled his hardening cock into her hands. She watched him as she licked along the stalk and around the head with her tongue. His eyes darkened, and his breathing grew deeper.

"Aw, baby. You don't have to do this."

She didn't answer him with words. Instead, she squeezed the base of him and raked his cock with her teeth. When he groaned, she squeezed his cock again, and then licked the drop of pre-cum from the slit at the top of his cock. He hissed out a breath. She began sucking just the cockhead into her mouth over and over, harder and harder before finally taking as much of his cock into her mouth as possible.

"Fuck! Your lips are stretched so tight around my cock. I love seeing you like this."

Beth grabbed his hands and put them on her head as she sank down and swallowed hard around his thick dick. He dug his nails into her scalp then began to fuck her face with his cock. She kept one hand at the base of him, so he wouldn't choke her and used the other hand to gently roll his balls. When she squeezed them lightly, he surged forward into her mouth, hitting the back of her throat and the top of her fist.

"Hell, yes! Do it again. I like feeling you deep-throat me, baby."

She grazed his balls with her nails and took him to the back of her throat. Mason growled.

"I'm going to come, baby. Swallow it all for me. Don't miss a drop of it."

She hummed her acceptance, and when he erupted with cum, she swallowed every drop of the salty liquid. Then she licked him clean and zipped him carefully back up. He sat with one hand on her head with his thrown back against the back of the couch. His breathing finally slowed to normal, and he opened his eyes.

"Thanks. I guess I needed that."

"I'd say you did. You look a little less tense." She giggled. "Now would you like something to eat?"

"I think I'll have a sandwich now."

Beth stood up and made a quick detour to the bathroom before returning to the kitchen and making sandwiches for them. She watched as Mason ate his with renewed vigor. She managed to eat most of hers but couldn't quite finish the rest of it.

Whatever was going on in the trial and had Mason on edge couldn't be good. She was curious, but she knew he really couldn't talk about it. Instead, she decided on a different topic they could worry about together.

"I haven't heard from the stalker. Is that good or bad?"

"I don't know, baby. His being quiet could mean he's gearing up for something. Remember to stay inside and don't open any of the doors."

"I won't." She hadn't meant to bring up a barrage of orders. She'd only meant to take his mind off of the trial.

"I'm going to have to be getting back, now. Depending on the trial, I'll be home around six again tonight. I'm not sure if Mac is planning on going out again or if we'll wait 'til Saturday night."

"I don't know either. He hasn't called me today. I figure he must be pretty busy."

"You have both of our numbers. You call if you need us." He held her face and kissed her before turning to leave. He picked up his briefcase where he'd left it in the kitchen.

Beth watched him leave before returning to the dining room to write. She heard his truck leave then lost herself in her writing.

Somewhere around three that afternoon, her phone rang. She picked it up and found it was Master Williams. She answered on the third ring.

"Hello?"

"Beth, how are you doing?"

"I'm fine. Is everything all right?"

"I'm worried about you, Larry being out and all. We haven't seen him around here."

"Well, I'm safe. Don't worry about me."

"Are you sure you don't want to come back to Dallas with us? You know we have a very secure home."

"I know. But my home is here, and I'm going to be going back to it as soon as my security system is installed."

"I hope you are using a reputable dealer."

"I'm using the one that the sheriff and his brother use. They're one of the best."

"Well, if you need us, you know where we are. We'll even come get you, Beth."

"Thank you, but I'm doing fine here. Bye."

"Good bye, Beth."

She laid the phone back down and resumed writing. When it rang again almost immediately, she nearly screamed. She started to answer it then remembered to check the number. It was an unlisted one. She stared at the number for several rings, and then let it go to voice mail.

Instead of calling Mac, she dialed her voice mail and waited on it to play back. The mechanical sound of her stalker's voice made her cringe as he spoke.

You're nothing but a slut. I was wrong about you, but I'm not wrong about knowing what you need. I can give you exactly what you need. I'll make sure you know who your true Master is. You'll beg me for forgiveness. Don't worry, Beth. I'll take good care of you. I'll take real good care of you.

Beth nearly dropped the phone. She quickly dialed Mac's number and waited as it went to voice mail.

"Mac, he called back. He's so angry. Please call me back." She hit *end* and waited with the phone in her hand for him to call her back.

When he didn't after nearly thirty minutes, she dialed Mason's number. It went to voice mail almost immediately. She repeated the same message to Mason that she'd left for Mac. Then she settled down and tried to concentrate on writing.

After another thirty minutes when neither man had called back, Beth grew angry. She was stuck out here without any help, and they weren't answering her messages. She was better off at home. Then the phone rang and she sighed in relief. It was Mac.

"I'm sorry, baby. I was in court testifying on Mason's case. I just got to where I could talk. Are you okay?"

"I guess. He was so angry this time."

"We got to him then. He should make a move, and we'll catch him when he does. I'll be home as early as I can, baby."

"Do you think he'll try something this weekend?"

"I'm counting on it, baby. We need to stop this bastard and soon."

"I want to go home and not be scared."

"Hang in there, Beth. It won't be long before everything will be okay."

She sighed when she heard the click of the phone indicating he'd hung up. She got up and got a glass of water then decided on making a cup of coffee instead. She waited for it to brew then returned to the dining room to settle down and write once again.

It wasn't long before she was totally wrapped up in her book. She heard something outside the window and started to check it out, but remembered that she didn't need to open the blinds. She waited to see if there would be another noise, but there wasn't, so she continued writing.

Several minutes later, a soft crunching sound jerked her head up from the computer. It sounded like a footstep outside in the gravel. She saved her work before running for the kitchen. She kept her eyes on the security unit at the back door. She figured it would tell her if someone was messing around out there. She heard another odd sound outside the door. She realized she had left her phone on the table in the other room and ran back to get it.

When she returned to the kitchen, she thought she saw a silhouette of someone at the backdoor through the curtain, but couldn't be sure. She contemplated calling Mac, but decided to wait and see if she heard or saw anything else.

After several minutes of standing there waiting for some noise or sound, she decided that whoever it was had left. She checked the clock on her phone and sighed in relief. It was nearly five. Mac would be home soon and Mason not long after that. She didn't like being out there all alone without any way to leave if she needed to. She, Mac, and Mason were going to have a talk.

She had just managed to settle down again when the crunch of tires alerted her that one of the men was home. She waited until they had made it all the way inside before launching herself out of the chair to the kitchen. Mac had no time to prepare before she was wrapped around him like a Velcro spider monkey.

"What's going on, baby?" He pulled her back enough that he could see her face.

"I think there was someone outside the dining room earlier. I could hear noises, but I couldn't really tell what they were."

"Why didn't you call me? I could have come on home."

"I was about to, but then when I didn't hear anything again, I figured you would be home soon anyway. It was probably only my imagination."

"Stay inside. I'm going to go check and see if I can see anything."

"Let me go with you. I'm tired of being cooped up inside. Please?"

"You stick with me, and don't wander off."

"I won't. I'll stay right with you." Beth nearly passed out when he agreed.

They walked out the back door and around the house to where she had heard the noise by the dining room. Sure enough, someone had been standing there. The grass was trampled below the windows. Mac walked all around the house with her in tow before they returned to the kitchen.

"Next time you hear anything, you call me. I might be able to catch him that way."

"I will. I'm sorry, Mac. I was afraid I was just imagining things."

"I'd rather be safe than sorry, baby. Especially where you are concerned."

"Do you know if Mason won his case or not? He was really down about it earlier today."

"I don't know, babe. He hasn't called me. We should hear from him soon, though. How about a beer? It's Friday, and barring anything major happening, I'm off for the weekend."

"Sounds good to me." She grabbed two out of the fridge and handed him one. They bumped cans and then drank.

"I thought we would stick around here tonight and then go out tomorrow night. Mason is probably going to be whipped."

"How about we order pizza in then?"

"Good idea. As soon as he calls so that we know when he'll get here, we'll call it in."

They chatted about his day as they waited on Mason to call or drive up. Thirty minutes later, the sound of someone driving up the drive alerted them to his arrival.

"Go stand in the dining room until I'm sure it's him, Beth."

She nodded and hid behind the dining room door to wait. Several seconds later, the back door opened and closed with the sound of Mac and Mason exchanging hellos. Beth exploded into the kitchen and hugged Mason.

"Did you win?"

"Yes and no. We won the case, but we didn't get the number of guilty verdicts we'd been going for. He was only found guilty on seven of the ten indictments of fraud."

"Does it matter really?"

"It could in determining his sentence length. We wanted as many as possible to make sure he did a good, long stretch of time."

"I'm sorry, Mason. You did your best though, I'm sure."

"It's okay, baby. How about a kiss?" He lifted her into his arms and kissed her hard on the mouth.

"We're going to order in pizza. Is that okay with you?" Mac asked.

"Good idea. I don't feel like going out or cooking. Pizza and beer."

Beth handed him a beer. He squeezed her ass before heading for the living room.

"I'm going to go change into something more comfortable. I'll be down in a few minutes."

Mac called in the pizza order of two large, thin-crust pizzas with everything. Beth figured she could pick off the olives. They were easy to see. When Mason made it back down a few minutes later, Mac climbed the stairs to change as well.

"How is your writing going?"

"I'm on track still. I wish I had more written, so I wouldn't worry if I got behind a little bit. Right now, holding to my schedule is about all I can manage."

"I guess it's not as easy to write somewhere different."

"No, I'm used to my things around me. Nothing is familiar here but my computer."

"We'll catch this guy soon, Beth. You'll see, everything will work out fine."

"I hope so. I'm tired of feeling like I'm in limbo or something."

"Who's in limbo?" Mac walked down the stairs into the living room.

"I am. I'm stuck here without a car to get around in and no one here but me. I need my car, Mac. I could have come to town and let you know that the guy had called again."

"That reminds me. I want to hear the message." He held out his hand.

Beth dug out her cell phone from her pants pocket and handed it to him. He listened then handed it to Mason to hear.

"I don't like it, Mac. He's angry. He's very unstable right now." Mason shook his head.

"He'll make a mistake like this. We'll catch him easier this way."

"I don't want Beth anywhere around this lunatic."

"Beth doesn't want to be anywhere around him either, but she's going to do whatever it takes to catch him." She glowered at both men for talking about her as if she weren't there.

"Baby, I'm worried that he'll get in a lucky hit or something." Mason ran his hand over her hair.

"Mason, I'll make sure we have plenty of help if something does come up. I figured we would go out on Saturday night. Silas and Jace will both be there around us looking for the guy. With the four of us watching out, she will be perfectly safe. Besides, the entire town is on the lookout for the man."

The doorbell rang, and Beth almost jumped into Mason's arms. He chuckled but held her while Mac checked to see if it were the pizza delivery man.

"Keep her out of sight, Mason."

Mason pulled her closer to him and wrapped his arms around her. Then he whispered in her ear.

"I'm going to return the favor later, baby."

Before she could say anything, Mac was back with two pizza boxes. He sat them on the coffee table and opened the top box.

"Grab a piece, Beth, or you might miss out."

"I'm going to get napkins. I'll be back." She hurried to the kitchen and grabbed paper towels for them to use as napkins.

When she returned, it was to find that the guys had switched on the TV to the news. They were waiting on her to sit down. She took her usual seat in the middle of the couch and grabbed a piece of the pizza as she did. They sat on either side of her with Mason's arm around her shoulders, and Mac's hand on her knee. They ate in silence as the news and weather came on.

Beth stopped after her third piece. She wasn't used to eating so much and immediately felt sleepy. She figured it had to be a combination of too much food and the beer.

"Guys, I'm going to go take my bath and get ready for bed in case I fall asleep early."

"Need some help?" Mason asked with a twinkle in his eye.

"No thanks. I can manage on my own." She grinned at them and hurried up the stairs.

It wasn't until she was relaxing in the bath that she thought about how easily she'd fallen into a routine with them. She needed to remember that this was temporary. She would be going home soon. It reminded her to check with Mason to see how they were doing on her house. She wasn't going to stay here indefinitely. Stalker or no stalker, she wanted to go home. She needed to go home before she lost more than her independence. She needed to go before she lost her heart as well.

Chapter Fifteen

Saturday morning, Beth woke to the feel of someone tickling the back of her neck. She swatted at them.

"You're awake. Come on, Beth."

"What?" She moaned and opened her eyes.

"There you are." Mac grinned over at her. "Mason is about to die to get in that sweet pussy of yours, but he didn't want to wake you up."

"You didn't have any trouble with waking me up, did you, Mac?" She groaned when he tugged on her hair.

"Don't move, Beth. I'm going to fuck that hot cunt from back here." Mason's husky voice sent chills down her spine.

"I think I'll watch you come, baby. I love seeing how you turn such a pretty shade of pink."

Mason lifted her leg and pulled it back over his hip, and then he lined up his sheathed cock with her slit and surged forward. Her eyes rolled back in her head when his huge dick lodged halfway inside her cunt. She couldn't help the slight yelp that emerged from her mouth as he squeezed into her body.

"You are so fucking tight. I can't see how I'm ever going to get all the way inside you, baby."

Mac ran a finger around and around her nipple then pinched it as Mason pulled out and thrust in again and again. She soon found herself pushing backward against his cock. The harder he thrust, the more she shoved back against him. He was soon pounding in and out of her pussy with Mac tugging and pulling on her tits.

"Hell, yeah, squeeze me like that again, baby."

She clamped down on Mason as Mac pinched and twisted her nipples. She could almost reach her climax. It was building but just out of reach. Mason's arm was around her waist, pulling her back on his thick cock. She grabbed hold of his arm and held on as she strained to reach orgasm. When he began to lose his rhythm, she knew he was almost there. She reached between her legs and pinched her clit. The little pinch there along with Mac twisting her nipples had her lunging for her orgasm in one quick jump. She screamed out Mason's name as he thrust in one more time and held still behind her. His arm nearly squeezed her breath from her.

She collapsed backward against Mason when he finally let go of her. Mac chuckled and pulled her toward him, so that Mason could deal with the condom. She groaned when he pulled out of her. Mac rubbed her back and kissed her forehead.

"Go back to sleep, baby. It's still early. No reason for you to have to get up yet."

She felt the bed dip, and Mason climbed back in to bury his face in the back of her neck.

"You're the best thing to wake up to, baby." He kissed her shoulder and then rested his hand on her thigh.

Beth relaxed between the two men and let herself drift. She really needed to get up and back to writing. She shouldn't be lounging around in the bed when she had a deadline ahead of her. Unfortunately, she couldn't convince herself to get up, and the next thing she knew she was dreaming.

* * * *

Mason pulled on his jeans before following Mac downstairs. They left Beth asleep in the bed. Mason was sure that after having come, she would sleep for at least another hour. Mac started the coffee, and Mason sat at the bar, rubbing a hand over his face. He was still sleepy.

He hadn't gotten much sleep the night before. They'd messed around until nearly midnight before heading to bed.

"She's going to look for someone else to do her security if they haven't started already."

"Fuck! I'll call them and have them start to work on it. I'll tell her they had to order what they needed and should start on it Monday morning." Mason sighed.

Mac poured the coffee as it was ready into two mugs. He handed one to Mason.

"That should work. I think she's scared of being out here all alone during the day. I don't know what to do about it though. She doesn't want to come in to the office and, frankly, I'm not there all the time to watch after her."

"We need to catch this guy then start working on winning her over." Mason sipped the coffee.

"That's going to be a massive undertaking as well. She's convinced she doesn't want to be with us. Every time one of us mentions anything that sounds like a relationship, she balks."

"I think that once all of this stalker business is taken care of, she'll be easier to convince. Right now, she's already scared. She's just extending it over to us as well."

Mac merely nodded. Mason could tell that Mac wasn't convinced that she would be able to make the leap at trusting them. He knew it would be a challenge, but he knew she was worth it.

"We're going to have to be on our toes tonight. I don't want someone to be able to grab her or even touch her." Mac turned his cup up and drained the last of his coffee.

"Don't worry. I'm going to be by her side all night.'"

"With Silas and Jace helping to keep watch, we should be able to find him fairly easily if he's going to be there. I can't imagine he'll not make a move as angry as he sounded in that message."

"So what is the plan for the night?" Mason asked.

"I figured we go out to eat again and then head over to the bar. I've already alerted Harold about what was going on. He's told his brother and his bouncer. I can't imagine the man getting to her. Larry shows his face and we'll have him."

"You know as a lawyer, I can get him off on the stalking charge without evidence that it was him. Otherwise all you'll have is circumstantial evidence."

"What in the hell are you suggesting, that I let him get his hands on her before I arrest him?"

"He at least needs to get close enough to threaten her within hearing distance of everyone around her."

"Fuck, Mason. Whose side are you on?"

"I want him convicted and sent to prison, Mac. I don't want him released to show back up when we least expect it. Right now, we're able to protect her because we're ready for him. What happens three or six months down the line when we're not looking for him?"

"Hell, you're right, but I don't want him touching her. I don't want him even close enough to touch her."

"Neither do I, Mac, but we have to be sure he goes to prison this time."

"Can you guarantee he won't go back to that damn insane asylum that let him out?"

"He showed the ability to think and plan when he set up surveillance cameras and bugged her house. I can't see a judge not ruling that he can stand trial." Mason ran a hand over his face.

A sound behind him alerted Mason that Beth was up and on her way into the kitchen. Mac must have noticed the sound as well because he grew quiet and stared toward the door. Mason turned around and smiled when she walked into the room with a disgruntled expression on her face. She was cute when she was grumpy.

"Why didn't you get me up when you two got up? I need to be writing."

"We didn't figure an hour would make much of a difference, and you needed the sleep, baby." Mason wrapped an arm around her waist and drew her over to the bar.

Mac handed her a cup of coffee and lifted an eyebrow at her muttered *thanks*.

"What would you like for breakfast, babe?" Mac asked.

"Nothing for me, thanks. I'm going to go start writing. I need to keep my word count up so that I'm on time with my book. I refuse to let that bastard make me late. I've never been late with a book." With that, she turned and walked toward the dining room with her coffee.

Mac shook his head and started breakfast. Mason left him to it and followed Beth into the other room. He sat at the table across from her, sipping his coffee. She looked up from booting up her computer, clearly annoyed.

"Are you going to sit and stare at me? If you are, you need to go somewhere else to stare. I can't write with you there."

"I'm waiting on breakfast. Mac's fixing it for all of us, and we're eating at the dining room table this morning."

She actually growled.

"Drink some more of your coffee, baby. You're grumpy."

She smiled sweetly and promptly ignored him as her computer signaled it was ready for use. She began to read. Mason just smiled and waited on Mac to appear with breakfast.

Several minutes later, Mac walked in with an omelet and some orange juice. He sat it next to her and disappeared only to return with two more plates. He handed one to Mason and sat down at the table with the other one. They began to eat.

Beth continued to ignore them but kept eyeing the omelet with obvious longing. He suppressed a smile when she finally gave in and scooted over to eat. He finished up his and grabbed Mac's empty plate as well. It was his turn to do the dishes. He raked, rinsed, and stuck them in the dishwasher. Then he snagged Beth's empty plate and juice glass and finished up the dishes.

When he returned to the other room, it was to find that Mac had disappeared and Beth was hard at the computer. He watched her for a few minutes then went in search of Mac. His cock had grown hard watching her with her tongue sticking out and her eyes rapt on what she was doing. It was sad when such an unsexy pose still managed to arouse him.

Mac was watching a Saturday-morning news show. No doubt he was checking the weather for the night. He wasn't leaving anything to chance. If the weather was bad, it would make it more difficult to be on alert with umbrellas and rain gear. He hadn't thought of that, but Mac evidently had.

"So, what's the verdict on the weather?"

"Looks like a fifty-fifty chance of rain. I don't like it, but it's what we have to work with. Let's pray for a dry evening."

"I'm all over that." Mason wouldn't leave anything to chance. Not where Beth was concerned. "What time are we leaving? I want to do a little paperwork to wrap up the case."

"I figure we'll go to eat around seven. That should put us hitting the bar around nine or nine fifteen."

"Come get me if you need me. I'm not doing anything that important."

Mason headed to the office to clean up the paperwork left over from the not-so-successful trial. He was still pissed off about that, but had to put it out of his mind to concentrate on keeping Beth safe. He was bound and determined that she would become their wife. He had wanted her since that fateful evening in the park all those years ago. There was no way he was going to give up this chance.

He wasn't sure how deep Mac was with her, but Mason knew he loved her. He would do anything for her. That included facing a crazy man down if need be.

Chapter Sixteen

Beth dressed in a sundress and grabbed a sweater since it was a little cool with the wind blowing. They were going out to eat and then over to the bar to dance for a while. She couldn't help but be nervous. There was a good chance that Larry would be there waiting on them somewhere. Would she recognize him after all this time? Surely he wouldn't have changed that much.

When she walked downstairs, the men were both sitting in the living room talking. They stopped when she walked farther into the room.

"Damn you look good." Mason stood up and walked over to give her a kiss.

"Very nice," Mac said as he, too, pulled her in for one as well. "We're going to have to beat them off with a stick, Mason."

"You both look really nice."

Both men were wearing navy blue slacks with light-blue button-down shirts. She could just imagine what their asses felt like beneath them. Her hands ached to find out now, but they were going to be leaving soon.

"Are you ready to go?" Mac asked.

"I guess. I'm really nervous, guys."

Mason wrapped his arms around her. "Baby, there's nothing for you to worry about. We're going to keep you safe."

"I know. I don't know what's wrong with me."

"It's facing something that happened to you in the past, Beth. I know it's hard to do, but it's over, and he can't hurt you again. I won't let him." Mac ran his hand through her hair and tugged on it. "Got it?"

She smiled. "Got it."

"Let's go then. I'm hungry." Mac led the way to the door.

Mason helped her up into the truck, and then helped her scoot over as he sat next to her. Mac climbed in on the other side in the driver's seat. He patted her knee then ran his hand a little ways up under her dress.

She grinned and slapped his hand. "No messing around while you're driving."

"That goes for you two, too. If I can't, then neither can you." He winked at her and started the truck.

They pulled into the steak house a few minutes later, and the men looked around before helping her out of the truck and escorting her to the door. No one jumped out at them or stopped them on the way inside. Beth breathed a sigh of relief, though, once they were seated in about the same spot as the night before.

"What are you going to have tonight, baby?" Mason asked.

"I don't know. I'm so nervous. I don't know that I can eat anything."

"You're going to eat something, babe. I'm not letting you go dancing unless you do. You'll need the energy." Mac pointed at her unopened menu.

Beth stuck her tongue out at him and picked it up. She looked over it and finally decided on a grilled chicken breast. It wouldn't be spicy or rich. She wanted something light. If she had to move fast, she didn't want to feel sluggish. That reminded her. She didn't need to drink much either.

"What are you thinking so hard about over there?" Mason squeezed her hand where it lay on the table.

"Just thinking that I shouldn't drink anything either. I need to have all my wits about me."

"Don't worry so much, babe. Mason and I will be right there with you. Plus, I have two deputies who are here and will be at the bar with us as well. You're well covered."

Once they had finished dinner, Mac paid the tab and Mason escorted her to the ladies' room. She freshened up and stared at herself in the mirror. Even she could see the nervousness in her eyes. She needed to get better control of herself. Taking a deep breath, Beth forced her nervous butterflies back into their box and walked back out to where Mac had joined Mason waiting on her.

"Ready?" he asked.

She nodded her head, and they left the restaurant to drive over to the bar. It wasn't that far, but neither of the men wanted to risk her being out in the open for as long as it would take to walk. Plus, if it rained, they would need to have the truck a little closer to keep from getting wet. She was thankful as she didn't think she could walk that far without having a nervous breakdown.

They parked in an open spot near the door. She wondered if they had arranged for it to be open. Mac could easily have done that being the sheriff. They walked into the bar, and the noise immediately took her breath away. Music blared in the back with the undertones of human voices calling out to each other. She felt the beat of the music in her chest as they wound their way around to a table that was empty in the back. It had to be Mac's doing again.

Mason seated her, and then each of the men sat on either side of her. Then Silas and Jace, wearing blue jeans and cowboy hats sat down across from them at the table.

"Beth, do you know Silas Atkins and Jace Vincent? Jace, Silas, this is Beth Hallmark."

They nodded at her and told her they were glad to meet her. She thought they looked familiar. She was sure she had seen them somewhere.

"How about a dance, baby?" Mason stood up and held her hand.

She looked over at Mac and then back at Mason. She stood up and allowed Mason to lead her to the dance floor. She kept close to Mason while they danced, afraid that at any moment, Larry would jump out and grab her.

"Relax, Beth. You're going to break you're so stiff. You're wound tighter than a spring on a watch."

"I'm sorry. I'm trying, but I'm scared."

"We've got you, Beth. I promise."

She sighed and relaxed a little into his arms. They danced through the next dance before returning to the table.

"Monopolizing her, Mason?" Mac asked with a grin.

"Can't help it. There's nothing better than her in your arms."

"I'll let you rest, Beth, but then it's my time."

She laughed at his serious expression. She sipped the drink that was sitting in front of her and began to relax. The rest of the evening passed in a blur of dancing and bathroom trips. Each time she had an escort of one of the men and one of the deputies. She felt almost like a royal princess.

Around midnight, Mac decided it was time to go. Nothing had happened all night, and everyone felt like Larry hadn't shown up. No one had seen him anywhere in town or at the bar. Mac clearly looked disappointed. Beth was relieved. She knew they needed to catch him, but she hoped it would be out in town somewhere and not around her.

They stepped outside into the night air, and Beth pulled her sweater tighter around her shoulders. The smell of rain was on the air, but so far, not a drop had fallen. No doubt Mac and Mason were happy about that. She was just glad not to get wet.

When they reached the truck, someone jumped out of nowhere and grabbed her arm.

"Beth, I need to talk to you. It's really important. Please, Beth, let me talk to you."

She screamed, and immediately Mac and Mason were all over Larry. He continued to yell as they dragged him away from her.

"Beth. I just want to tell you I'm sorry. I'm so fucking sorry. I was crazy. I needed help. I'm so sorry. Please forgive me, Beth."

Mac and Mason turned him over to Silas and Jace. They carted him off to their vehicle, leaving Mac and Mason to see about her.

"Are you okay, baby? Fuck, I'm sorry. I promised you he wouldn't touch you. We weren't paying enough attention." Mac checked her over. He looked at her arm where Larry had grabbed her.

"There's going to be a bruise there. I'm sorry."

"It's okay. You got him. That's all that matters. It's over with now. Right?" She was shivering all over now. Whether it was from the cool night air or shock setting in, she didn't know.

"Let's get you home, baby." Mason helped her up in the truck, being careful of her arm.

They arrived back at the house just as the rain began to fall. Mac ran and unlocked the door while Mason got out the umbrella and helped her cross the short path from the truck to the back door.

Mac immediately pulled her into his arms and hugged her. He buried his face in her hair and rubbed her back with his big hands.

"How about a nice hot bath?" he asked.

"I'll go run it for you." Mason kissed the top of her head and hurried off.

"It's over, right, Mac?"

"It's over, baby. We'll charge him for stalking and a few other things. It should be enough to put him back in the loony bin if not jail."

"I want to go home, Mac."

"Shh. Not yet, baby. As soon as they finish your alarm system, you can go back. They got the parts in yesterday and are going to be working on it first thing Monday morning."

"You promise?"

"I promise. Are you in a hurry for some reason?"

"I miss my things around me. Your house is wonderful. I love it, but my things are important to me. I feel normal around them."

"You don't feel normal here?"

"I just feel like I'm visiting, which is what I'm doing."

"It won't be long, Beth. Just a little longer."

She heard the longing in his voice, and it burned in her heart. She wanted them so badly, but there was no way a relationship could work between the three of them. She couldn't give them the trust that they deserved. She just didn't have it in her anymore. Larry had taken so much from her. She didn't think she would ever get any of it back.

* * * *

When Beth finally got out of the tub, she was sure that she had prune skin from having soaked so long. The men had come to check on her twice. She'd kept adding warm water until she finally admitted that she had to get out.

She was startled when she walked out into the room wearing nothing but a towel by the sight of two totally nude men waiting by the bed for her. She smiled and dropped her towel.

"Fuck, you're beautiful." Mason walked over and bent over her for a kiss.

She responded with her lips and teeth. He groaned and thrust his tongue in and out of her mouth, imitating what he wanted to do to her. Mac pushed in behind her, grinding his rock-hard cock into her lower back.

"Let's get you to bed where we can take good care of you." Mac pulled her gently from Mason's kiss.

She let him lead her to the bed where he turned her around and had her sit down on the edge. Mason walked around to the other side of the bed and reached over to carefully pull her back to the center where she lay down and waited for the men to descend on her. Mac was first. He knelt on the bed next to her and began to massage her shoulders, moving to her arm and making sure not to touch her tender patch.

Mason was next. He started at her feet and worked his way up, touching and teasing every square inch of her skin. When he reached her pussy, he stopped and settled himself between her legs. Anticipation built as they stared at each other. He slowly lowered his head and focused his attention on her pussy lips. She nearly screamed when he sucked them in and swirled them around in his mouth. Then he tugged on them as he released them.

Mac got her attention again when he sucked a nipple into his mouth and flattened it against the roof of his mouth to lick it over and over. Pleasure shot from her nipple to her clit. When he nipped it, she yelled out and dug her fingers into the covers. He divided her attention by plucking at the other nipple with his fingers. She squirmed between the two men. They were equally driving her crazy.

Her pussy was being eaten as thoroughly as if she were a set of barbecue ribs good enough to gnaw the bones. Mason was doing everything but gnaw her bones. He stabbed her pussy with his stiffened tongue then ran it up and down her slit, gathering her juices. He entered her with two fingers and began to slowly fuck them in and out of her cunt. About the same time that he found her hot spot, Mac twisted both her nipples at the same time.

Beth bucked, screaming out their names as they continued to torment her. Mason stroked over her sweet spot again and again. Mac plucked and pinched her nipples, and then licked them in a soothing motion.

Nothing could compare to their loving when she was truly relaxed and at ease with everything. All of the tension from the last few weeks began to melt away as they drove her closer and closer to climax. Pleasure swirled in a kaleidoscope of colors around her as she threw her head back and screamed.

Mason sucked in her clit between his teeth and rubbed it with the flat of his tongue while Mac pinched and pulled on her nipples at the same time. She grabbed at his hair, pulling him down to her breasts as she bucked beneath them.

Just as she thought her climax was over, Mason lifted her legs over his arms and plunged into her spasming cunt. He grunted when he only made it halfway. He pulled out and drove in again and again until he was as far in as he could go. His thick dick was lodged deep in her cunt. Her pussy burned with the stretch around his cock.

He groaned and pulled out to push back in. Each stroke of his cock sent him rasping over her hot spot once again. She groaned. When she turned her head, Mac took her mouth with his in a soul-searing kiss. She gasped for breath as he thrust his tongue in and out in a quick-jabbing rhythm.

Mason tunneled in and out of her swollen pussy, building the pressure once again. She didn't see how she could ever climax a second time so soon, but Mason was driving her up once again.

Mac pulled back from their kiss and rubbed noses with her before rising to his knees and tapping her lips with the spongy head of his purple-colored cockhead. It looked angry and needy bobbing out from his body. She licked her lips and opened her mouth for him to plunge in as far as he could go. Beth wrapped her hand around the base to keep him from choking her. Then she licked and sucked as he fucked her mouth.

With each slide down her throat, she swallowed around him, earning herself a curse. He dug his hands into her hair and pulled on it as he tunneled in and out of her mouth. She moaned around him, and he cursed again.

"Fuck, baby. That feels unbelievable."

Mason changed his angle, and soon she was racing toward her orgasm so fast she became dizzy.

Mac cursed when she swallowed around him twice in a row. He pulled his cock out with an audible *pop*.

"No you don't. I'm not coming in your mouth. I'm getting a piece of that sweet pussy when Mason is through with you."

Mason continued thrusting in and out of her with his thick dick. Lights exploded in front of her as she shot over in climax. Her scream was cut short when Mac covered her mouth with his and swallowed it as his own.

Mason shouted out as he came, spilling his seed in the condom. He slowly lowered her legs and pulled out before collapsing to the side. Beth fought for breath as Mac took Mason's place.

He fitted his sheathed cock at her entrance and plunged inside of her all the way to her cervix. She called out his name as he pulled back out and thrust again. His long dick was perfect for bumping her cervix, and after Mason had stretched her with his thick cock, Mac could easily tunnel in and out of her pussy. He adjusted his angle and soon bumped her clit with each shove of his cock.

He grunted as he pummeled her cunt over and over. She could tell he was close and clamped down on his dick with every stroke he made.

"Fuck, baby. Your cunt is squeezing me like a warm, wet fist. I swear you're going to milk me dry. Aw—hell, yes!" He speeded up but lost his rhythm as he tunneled to the edge of climax. Beth pumped her hips up to meet his thrusts, sending him into a tailspin that she knew would end in his coming deep inside of her. When he did, he held himself stiff above her for several long seconds before falling over on top of her. He caught himself with his hands before smothering her.

Sweat dripped from his brow to her breasts. She cupped either side of his face in her hands and stared up into his eyes still dark with arousal as he slowly recovered. His heavy breathing covered up the sound of her more shallow pants. Then he pulled out of her with a groan and padded into the bathroom.

Mason was there covering her with the sheet and stroking her body to help her calm down enough to sleep.

"I'm sorry, baby." Mac climbed back in bed.

"What for?"

"You didn't come. That was my fault. I let you suck my control away. I couldn't hold off long enough."

"Mac, if I had come again, I might have passed out. I am more than satisfied. I don't think my body can take much more than twice after everything that happened tonight." She snuggled up to him.

"I'll make it up to you."

Beth giggled. She couldn't believe that he was so upset over her not climaxing. In the past, no one cared if she even came once. It was refreshing and strangely endearing. She wiggled between them until they both growled at her to make her nest and settle down. She finally felt like the past was in the past, and they had helped her put it there. If only she could regain her trust. She could have it all with them, if she would learn to trust once again.

Chapter Seventeen

The next Friday her house was finally finished and ready for her to move back into. Mac and Mason both tried to talk her into waiting until Sunday afternoon, but she was anxious to get back to normal. Plus, if she was honest with herself, she needed to put some space between her and them. They were beginning to convince her that they could make things work between them.

"Are you sure, baby?" Mason carried her suitcase into her bedroom and set it on the bed for her. "We can take it back."

"I'm sure, Mason. We've been over this a thousand times." She carried her computer into her office and set it on the desk.

She looked around and grimaced. Despite the men having cleaned it all up, she could feel the intrusion in her private space. She hoped she would be able to get over it. Otherwise, she would have to move. There was no way she could work and be uncomfortable. Larry had a lot to answer for. She hoped they sent him back to the hospital. He belonged there. What he had done was sick as far as she was concerned.

Mac walked in the office and wrapped his arms around her.

"I double-checked everything, and it all works fine. Are you sure you remember how to work it all? I can go over it with you again."

"I'm sure, Mac. Thanks."

They walked out of the office and found Mason in the living room sitting on her love seat. She didn't have a couch because the room wouldn't hold one. It was a cozy little room that served her purposes well. She never had visitors, so she didn't need much in the way of furniture.

"I guess we should be going, then." Mason stood up but didn't look ready to leave.

"You have our numbers programmed into your phone under speed dial. Just push one for me, two for Mason, and nine for the sheriff's office. Don't hesitate to call for anything, baby." Mac stuck his hands in his pockets.

"I'll walk you to the truck." She headed for the door only to be brought up short when Mason pulled her backward into his arms. He nuzzled her neck and breathed in deeply.

"I don't think I'll ever get enough of smelling you. Go out with us tomorrow night, baby."

"I think we need a week to cool off some, Mason. Just a week. I need to get back into my rhythm. Please?" She pleaded with him with her eyes.

Mac crowded her into Mason. "One week, baby. Then you let us court you. We want you for more than a week or a month, baby. I think you know that."

"You haven't exactly said anything."

Mac cursed and held her face between his beefy hands. "You mean the world to us. We want you to move in and live with us. I'm not asking for anything more right now, because I don't want you to run away from us. Just give us the opportunity to take you out and win your trust."

"Mac, you're asking a lot of me. I don't know if I can do that."

"Give us a chance. Next week. We'll back off for a week."

"Okay." She sighed. She couldn't say no.

Mason's sigh behind her heated the back of her neck. She hadn't realized he'd been holding his breath on her answer.

"Come on, Mason. Let's let her get settled in." Mac backed away from her and nodded toward the door. "Don't forget to set the alarm after we leave, Beth."

"I won't. She followed them to the door and kissed both of them briefly on the lips before waving them off. Then she set the alarm and headed for the bedroom to unpack.

After putting away her clothes and dropping her dirty clothes in her hamper, Beth took stock of her kitchen and made a grocery list for in the morning. Then she wandered into the office and set her computer and notes back up like they belonged. After thirty minutes of fiddling, she settled down to write. Only she couldn't get into her groove. She didn't feel comfortable in her office anymore. She'd been spied on there.

Finally, she called it a night and took a quick shower before climbing into bed. When she turned off the light, she lay there a long time unable to sleep. The smoke detector flashed a light every once in a while, reminding her that there had been a camera there at one time watching her in her bed. The things it had seen embarrassed her and made her mad all at the same time.

She tossed and turned for over an hour before finally getting up and mixing a light drink. She carried her laptop to the kitchen and settled at the table. After a few false starts, she finally got going again. The next time she looked up, dawn was creeping through her windows. She yawned and stretched. She wasn't really sleepy, just a little tired.

After saving a dozen times in a dozen different ways, Beth got up and got dressed. She would get an early start by going to the grocery store as soon as they opened. Then she would move what she needed to write into the kitchen and use the table. She could eat at the bar. Maybe after a while she could move back into her office. As for her bedroom, she'd sleep on the loveseat for a while. She was short enough that it wouldn't be too uncomfortable. The good thing about that was that she would be close to her computer if she got up in the middle of the night to write or got sleepy and needed a nap.

Two hours later, she headed to the grocery store. When she arrived, she got out and had the strangest feeling someone was watching her. When she turned around to look, Mac's truck sat across the street with him standing by the front of it. He waved at her then continued toward the court house. She smiled to herself and walked into the store to do her shopping. At least he wasn't following her to be sure she was okay.

It would be bad to get rid of one stalker only to pick up another one. With that thought, she began filling her buggy with groceries.

* * * *

Early Friday evening, the doorbell rang at a quarter to seven. She sighed and hurried to let them in. She was mostly dressed, but still needed to put on her shoes and put in earrings.

"You're early."

"We know, but we couldn't wait." Mason grinned down at her and pulled her in for a kiss.

"He couldn't wait. I was waiting just fine." Mac took his turn at her mouth.

"Says the guy who had the truck running when I walked outside."

"It's nippy outside. I wanted it to be warm for Beth."

She shook her head and smiled. They were so like little boys sometimes. She cared about them deeply. She might even be in love with them. She just didn't think it would work. Not as long as she couldn't trust them. They would need her submission. It was just how they were.

"Hey, why the frown?" Mason ran a thumb over her lips.

"Sorry, just thinking too hard. I need to put on my shoes. I'll be right back." She hurried into the bedroom to slap on some earrings and slip into her shoes.

She took a quick look at herself in the mirror and decided she would do. When she stepped back out into the living room, the men were standing by her makeshift desk. They looked up when she walked in.

"You look great, Beth." Mason smiled at her and held out his hand.

"Why are you writing in here, baby?" Mac asked.

"I just can't get past that he bugged my office. I'll get back in there in a few days. I'm just making do for now."

Mac just nodded, took her elbow and headed for the door. Mason followed behind them. She turned to look at him over her shoulder. He smiled at her and blew her a kiss. When they got to the truck, Mac opened the door and helped her inside. Then he got in on the other side and started the engine while Mason climbed in next to her and shut the door.

"Feel up to the diner tonight? I thought we'd eat there and then go for a drive."

"Sure. I haven't seen Mattie in a long time. I bet she's forgotten all about me by now."

"Not a chance, baby. No one could forget you." Mason kissed her on the cheek and squeezed her hand.

Mac settled one hand on her thigh as they drove toward the Riverbend Diner. When he pulled in out front, he squeezed her knee then got out. Mason helped her down before escorting her to the door. Mac opened it for her, and she walked in to be surrounded by well-wishers. It overwhelmed her, and she was thankful when Mac cleared them out so she could breathe.

"Everyone just wants you to know they were worried about you. This is a close-knit community, and you're one of their own." Mason held her chair for her.

"Beth! It's so good to see you in here. I've missed you." Mattie squeezed her shoulder. "What can I get you guys to drink?"

They gave their drink orders then looked over the menus. When returned with their drinks, they were ready to place their orders.

"How is the writing coming?" Mason asked.

"Everything is working out fine. I just got a late start until I moved to the kitchen."

"Have you even slept in your bed yet?" Mac asked without looking at her.

"Um, no." She looked off toward the cash register.

"You're sleeping on that loveseat?" Mason looked as if he would choke.

"I don't sleep that much anyway. I mostly write. I'll get back to my bed in a little while. I just can't do it right now. It's all too fresh."

"I hate the idea of you sleeping on that uncomfortable thing."

Mac nodded his head. "I feel the same way. Why don't you come back to our place, Beth? You were fine there."

"Guys, I have to be able to live on my own or I'll never feel good about myself again. Give me some time."

Mac sighed and nodded his head. Mason's mouth thinned into a line before he too nodded his head.

"Doesn't mean we have to like it," Mac said.

"Fair enough."

Their food came out, and they talked about safe things while they ate. After splitting a piece of pie three ways, they loaded back up in the truck, and Mac headed out of town. Beth didn't ask where they were going. She figured they would tell her eventually.

"Baby, we wanted to talk to you about us." Mason indicated the three of them with his hand.

"I don't understand."

"We thought we'd drive down to the lake and sit and talk it all out."

"Just a minute, Mason. We're almost there now." Mac maneuvered the truck down the curvy road until he reached the picnic area near the lake. He parked and cut the engine. Then he turned toward her.

"Baby, we love you. We want you to be our wife. I know that's jumping way ahead, but we think you should know what our intentions are."

Mason turned her toward him. "I love you, baby. I want us to be a family. I know you're scared, but that's okay. We've got all the time in the world to convince you we're serious and to relieve your fears."

Beth opened and closed her mouth several times, trying to figure out what to say. She was totally blindsided by this. She knew they had wanted her to move in with them, but marriage? That was out there for her. She couldn't even promise them a real relationship, much less marriage.

"You're not saying anything," Mason said.

"I'm not sure what to say. I don't think this is possible, guys. I care about you very much. You know my past. I'm not sure I will ever be able to trust someone enough to do the whole D/s thing again. I won't lie to you. I miss it. I found something in it that truly completed me, but that takes a good bit of trust, and I am scared to even try now. I'm scared I'll totally freak out. That wouldn't be something I could easily get over."

"We're not asking you to live that type of life, Beth. We know you're unsure about that." Mac took her hand in his. "We're asking for a chance at a normal relationship."

"You can't change who you are, Mac. You'll eventually come to resent me for not being able to give you what you need. You need that just like I need to write."

"I think you're wrong, Beth. Please just give us a chance. Don't shut us out without trying to make this work. Even if it's not what we want right away, we don't want to lose you."

Mason huffed out a breath and turned her toward him. Before she knew what his intentions where, he pulled her into a kiss. As kisses went, it was almost a punishing kiss it was so intense. He ate at her mouth with his. His fingers dug into her scalp as he sucked her tongue into his mouth to tease with his. When he lightly bit it, she moaned and wrapped her hand in his hair. She held him there with it as she returned the kiss.

Finally, he pulled back, leaving her gasping for air. She searched his face for what he was feeling. Finding nothing to give her a hint, she sighed.

"I can't promise anything, Mason. I just can't."

"All we're asking is that you try. We want to try to be a family. I know you don't want to move in right now. I can sort of understand that, but let us date you and claim you. That's all we want right now if that is all you're willing to give."

Beth bit her lower lip, trying to decide what to do. She didn't think she was going to be able to say no. They had said they loved her. She didn't see how in such a short period of time, but if the truth be told, she thought she was in love with them, too. She just hadn't admitted it to herself, yet. Was she admitting it now?

"I'll try, but don't expect anything."

She immediately found herself engulfed in a bear hug from Mason on one side and snuggled from Mac on the other. She finally managed to get them to release her so she could breathe.

"We'll take real good care of you, Beth. You'll see." Mason seemed over the moon.

"We'll go slow and do things at your pace," Mac assured her.

A few minutes later, Mac started the truck and headed back to town. When they pulled up outside her house, she felt the tension return. She had to get past it. This was her home for goodness sake. She either had to move beyond the entire episode, or she would have to move. She didn't want to move.

Mac and Mason both got out of the truck to walk her inside. She remembered the security system just in time to disengage it. First Mac pulled her into his arms and kissed her. He kissed her as if he might not see her again for a long time. When he finished, Mason took her from him and gently kissed her at the corners of her mouth before giving her a good-night kiss.

"We'd like for you to come over tomorrow for a cookout. We thought we would grill steaks and watch a movie."

"Umm…"

"Say yes, baby." Mason rubbed her arms up and down.

"What time?"

"How about five? We'll eat around six thirty, and then watch a movie," Mac chimed in.

"Okay. That sounds good. What should I bring? Bread?"

"Nothing. We'll have it all covered," Mason said.

Mac hugged her one more time then with Mason right behind him. She walked them back to the door and locked them out. She reset the alarm and headed for the bedroom. She quickly took a shower before changing into her sleep shirt and curling up on the love seat. After about fifteen minutes, Beth fell asleep.

Chapter Eighteen

Beth hurried through her bath and got dressed in a rush. She had lost track of time while writing. She was going to be late. She climbed into the Pathfinder and backed out of her drive. She headed for Mac and Mason's house. When she pulled into the drive, both men walked out of the house at the same time.

"We were beginning to wonder if you were going to show up." Mac helped her out of the car.

"Sorry, I lost track of time."

"Writing, huh?" Mason grinned at her.

"Ah, yeah. I forgot to set my alarm to remind me."

"Next time we'll remember to call," Mac said.

"I guess if you want me to be on time, you're going to have to. I'm not used to going anywhere and needing to be on time unless I'm out of town."

"When is your next trip out of town?" Mason guided her to the couch.

"Not until spring."

"So the winter months you are basically holed up in your house writing." Mac sat down on the other side of her.

"That's about it unless my agent or publisher wants to see me for some reason. Sometimes I end up with a trip to New York, but I haven't heard anything."

"How often do you go to Dallas?" Mason asked.

"Not very often. If my agent is there visiting her family, then I might drive there for a meeting."

Mac stood up and walked back toward the kitchen. "I'm going to get a glass of wine for you."

Mason wrapped an arm around her shoulders and pulled her in for a soft kiss. He didn't press her, just kissed her and let her go. Then Mac was back with her glass of wine. She took a sip and smiled. It was her favorite. But of course he would know because he'd been all through her house.

"How do you like your steak?" Mac asked.

"Medium is fine."

He nodded and left her with Mason once again. She shifted so that she could see him. He smiled and took her hand.

"So, are you on schedule?"

"I should be finished with the book by Sunday night. Then I have to revise it."

"How long will that take?"

"Oh, depends. Usually it takes me about two weeks. Then I send it in."

"So you'll make your deadline without any trouble."

"I should. Provided nothing happens to slow me down." She lifted her eyebrows at him.

Mason laughed. "You should worry about us. We just might whisk you away for a long weekend somewhere."

"Make it in two weeks, not before. I need to finish this book and get it out of my hair. I have memories with it and don't want to have to look at it much more."

Mason's smile sobered. "I can understand that. How about we plan a trip the weekend you shoot it out the door?"

"Um, I guess. Where would you want to go?"

"We'll talk about it later. Maybe Austin."

"I haven't been there in years and years."

"Hey, you guys! The steaks are ready."

Mason stood up and pulled her to her feet. They walked into the dining room, and Mason seated her at the head of the table. They sat on either side of her. The three of them ate while they chatted about mutual acquaintances and some of the weird things Mac had dealt with lately. Once they had finished, Mac led her into the living room and turned on the TV while Mason dealt with the dishes.

"You know if you would let me help him we could be finished in no time." Beth didn't like not helping clean up.

"Nope, it's his turn to deal with the dishes, and my turn to have time with you."

Mac pulled her back into his arms so that they both could see the TV. He spent his time nibbling her neck and nuzzling behind her ear. She kept squinching her neck because he was tickling her.

"You're awful ticklish there."

"I can't help it. You're tickling me there. Cut it out."

"I can't help it. You're so fun to tickle." Mac licked up her neck then sucked in her earlobe.

"I thought we were watching a movie."

"We are as soon as Mason makes it back. Settle down, and enjoy the commercials."

She giggled at that but wiggled until she was comfortable between Mac's legs. He grunted a time or two while she was getting her nest made. There was no mistaking the bulge pressing against the top of her ass. It reminded her that they were very sexual men, and she was almost certain they would end up in bed together before the night was over. She wouldn't be disappointed either.

Mason finally walked in, carrying two beers in one hand and her wine in the other.

"I freshened up your wine, baby."

"Thanks, I don't usually drink very much."

"You just ate, another glass shouldn't hurt," Mac said.

"Okay, time for the movie." Mason switched on the DVD player and pressed play.

For the next hour and a half, they watched an action thriller with plenty of sex and car chases. She couldn't help but clap when the good guys got the bad guys. She had rooted for them the entire movie. Mac and Mason kept watching her and laughing at her enthusiasm.

When it was over, Mac shook his head and chuckled. "I don't think I've ever watched a movie with anyone who had as much fun as you did."

"I hope I didn't ruin it for you. No one ever likes to go to the movies with me."

Mason grinned. "I can see us at the movies with her one night and having them kick us out for being too rambunctious."

"I'm not that bad."

Mac and Mason exchanged looks and nodded their heads that yes she was. Beth pouted and crossed her arms.

"None of that, missy." Mac picked her up and twirled her around the room. "Would you like to dance?"

"Here?"

"Sure. We have a good sound system."

Mason walked over and fiddled with something in the bookcase, and music flowed through the room. Mac slow danced with her, holding her close to him. She could feel the rigid outline of his straining cock. Then Mason scooted in behind her and she felt another cock straining at the zipper. He rubbed it against her lower back as they moved around the floor. They danced through two songs before Mason pulled her out of Mac's arms and took over the next two dances.

Beth thoroughly enjoyed herself as they danced her from one end of the living room to the other. Then Mason was picking her up and carrying her up the stairs. She relaxed in his arms, so he wouldn't drop her. When they made it to the bedroom, Mac took her from Mason and kissed her before letting her slide down his body to stand on her own.

"Baby, we want to make love to you. Will you let us?"

"Um, I think that since I let you bring me up here that I'm okay with it."

"No, we want to love you at the same time," Mason said.

"I want in that tight ass of yours, and Mason wants to fuck your pretty pussy." Mac didn't mince words. He told her exactly what they wanted. Now she understood.

"I've never, um done that before."

"You've had butt plugs though, right?"

"Yes."

"We'll go slow and prepare you, baby," Mason reassured her.

"I want you both inside of me, but I'm scared."

"Don't be scared, Beth. We'll stop anytime you tell us to. Just give us a chance to show you how good it can be."

Mac cupped her face in his hands and drew her in for an easy, sensual kiss. He licked along the seam of her lips. When she opened, he licked around her mouth and twined his tongue with hers. He pulled back and stared intently down into her eyes. She couldn't deny him anything.

"Yes. I'll try."

"Good girl." He began unbuttoning her long-sleeve blouse.

Mason knelt at her feet and directed her to step out of her shoes as he removed them. Then he unfastened her jeans and lowered them to the floor. She stepped out of the jeans. This left her with nothing on but her underwear once Mac removed her blouse. She was vaguely aware that Mason folded her clothes and placed them on the chair.

"You're beautiful, Beth," Mac said.

He held her hands away from her body and stared at her from head to toe. Mac walked up behind her and unhooked her front-closure bra and peeled one cup at a time away from her breasts. Then he pulled her arms behind her back, using the straps from the bra. When he kept them like that while Mason walked up and began playing with her nipples, she didn't think anything of it. She had enough give to move her hands some, so it didn't bother her.

Mac continued to play with her nipples. He bent down and licked first one then the other. Mason tugged on her arms, and then there was the feel of silk against her neck. He wrapped it around her face and covered her eyes with it before securing it behind her head. For a second, she panicked but quickly recovered. It was Mac and Mason. They wouldn't hurt her.

Mac pulled on her nipples then let go of them and let them pop back. She drew in a deep breath. It felt good to be able to enjoy a little bondage. It wasn't hard core, but it was good just the same.

Mac turned her around, and fingers plucked and pinched her nipples. She assumed it was Mason since he'd been behind her originally. The little bite of pain was very arousing to her. She liked her sex slightly rough, but not overly so. Being tied up brought back memories of life before the incident and how much she enjoyed the bondage play. Would she ever be able to go back to that?

"How are you doing, baby?" Mac's voice.

"Good. I'm good."

"Excellent." Mason's voice.

They led her over to what turned out to be the bed, and one of them helped her to climb up on it. She knelt there waiting for whatever came next. Nothing moved for a long time, and then she heard the whisper of material around her. She tried to make out what it was, but she couldn't. Then someone climbed up on the bed with her.

Skin slid against her back. It had been the sound of clothes coming off. Whoever was with her on the bed was nude. She shuddered when he tugged on her hair. Then the bed dipped again and another body pressed against her front. She sniffed and knew Mac was behind her and Mason in front of her. She could tell the difference in their scents. Where Mason smelled like fresh pine and summer nights, Mac was a more woodsy musk.

Then they were rubbing her all over. Hands massaged her breasts then kneaded them. More hands were rubbing down her pelvis to settle at her trimmed pussy. A mouth sucked on one of her nipples while the hand at her pussy moved further downward. Fingers dipped into her dripping pussy and massaged her there.

Beth moaned as they seemed to touch her everywhere that added to her arousal. She strained to push her chest closer to the mouth that was nipping and sucking on her nipples. She thrust her pelvis toward the hand there in hopes of impaling her starving pussy on a finger or two. They pulled away and someone popped her on the ass. She drew in a deep breath. She'd crossed a line and received her punishment. This was what she had missed, the exchange.

Now someone removed her binding from her arms and gently moved them back to her sides. Hands massaged her shoulders until they were no longer stiff feeling. She was pulled back into someone's embrace. Once again she smelled musky woods. It was Mac. He pulled and plucked at her nipples, adding just a little pain to enhance her pleasure. Then he was urging her forward. She found that Mason's body was in front of her. She widened her legs and straddled him as she crawled up his body.

When she found his sheathed cock, she squeezed it lightly. The hiss of breath was the only sound she heard. Then she was directed to take him into her pussy. She lifted up and let him rub it up and down her slit until he was pushing in small increments into her pussy. She tried to plunge down on him, but he spanked her hip and pulled back. She whimpered. A soft chuckle reached her ears.

Once again, he positioned his dick at her opening, only this time, he pulled her down on him in one quick jab.

"Oh, God!"

Then he was thrusting into her over and over until he was all the way inside of her. His thick cock stretched her pussy wide. She embraced the slight burn that he gave her with his massive girth. He continued to push up and pull out over and over until Mac's hand pressed her gently down onto Mason's chest. Then Mason wrapped his arms around her to hold her there. She struggled for just a few seconds to ascertain that she was indeed held tightly and securely.

She felt the cold addition of lube at her back entrance. The little rosette puckered at the temperature of the stuff. A finger twirled it around and around her dark hole, pressing inward with every pass over it.

He played with her for several seconds before finally pressing into her with his finger. The pressure was slight, but she knew it would get worse with the second finger. He pumped the first finger in and out of her until she was pushing back with each plunge of his finger. More lube coated her hole, and he added the second finger. This one burned. She pressed outward and breathed through the heat.

He pushed forward and pulled out until he was satisfied she was open enough to take a third finger. More lube, and the third finger pushed in with the other two. She whimpered.

"Shhh." Hands soothed up and down her back.

She breathed out and pushed out to let the three fingers inside her. They made it past the resistant ring to surge forward. He slowly pumped them in and out of her. She soon pushed back on him as he pushed forward. Then they were removed, and lube pressed in her back hole before the unmistakable feel of Mac's cock pressed against her dark hole. He pushed inward as she pushed out and panted through the pain of admitting him inside her past the resistant ring.

"Oh, God, oh, God." She chanted it over and over as she tried to breathe around the pain. Then there was nothing but pressure that nearly choked her.

Once he made it inside, he surged forward and stilled to let her adjust to the fullness of two cocks inside her body. It was unreal–surreal. Beth tried to pull up off of Mason and push back on Mac, then down on Mason and off of Mac. She needed them to move. They had to move.

"Easy, baby. Let us do the work. Just feel." Mac's voice calmed her to the point that she was able to let them take over.

They set up a rhythm so that they slid over one another, sending chills up her spine from the friction it created. She was full of cock at all times. It thrilled her as the pleasure-pain washed over her. Her pussy stretched to its limit and her ass full of cock gave a whole new meaning to the words fucked seven ways to Sunday.

Again and again they thrust in and out of her. A new kind of pressure began to build inside of her. It spiraled upward until she thought she would explode with it. She held on tight to Mason's arms as he held her hips and pushed up inside of her.

Mac tunneled in and out of her ass as his hands held her waist, pulling her back onto his cock. She shuddered when fire ignited inside her bloodstream. Molten and burning, it circulated through her body, sending the pleasure even higher. Then Mac ran his hand around her to find her clit. He pressed his finger on it over and over. She screamed as her climax hurtled her into the heavens. Stars exploded in her head until she was blind from it.

"Fuck! Squeeze me baby," Mason called out. "Yeah, just like that."

"It's like a silk glove squeezing my dick. Aw, hell. I'm going to come."

Beth felt them spasm inside of her as they filled the condoms with their cum. Nothing would ever come close to what they had shared this night. The sensations were all that more stimulating and intense because of the blind fold.

She collapsed on top of Mason. He reached around and removed the silk scarf, kissing her all over her face.

Mac groaned and leaned his head against her lower back. She felt sweat pool there. Hers or his, she didn't know. Maybe it was a combination of both of theirs. Something amazing had taken place, and it involved her heart. She had no doubt she loved them now. What was she going to do about it? What could she do about it? Aftershocks of pleasure tightened her womb. Mason grunted. Mac groaned.

Then Mac pulled out of her and left them there for a few seconds. When he came back, they both helped her off of Mason and it was his turn to leave. She rolled over and wrapped herself around Mac. She needed to feel something solid after all the flying she'd done. Mac was solid and Mason her anchor. They held her close while she rethought her life.

Chapter Nineteen

The next two weeks passed by quickly. Beth spent a good number of her nights with Mac and Mason. Despite her lack of night writing time, she managed to keep on track. She seemed to be writing easier and just perhaps, better than ever before.

This was the weekend they planned to go to Austin. She'd turned in her manuscript and was ready to celebrate. She had a couple of errands to run Friday morning before they were leaving late that afternoon. She already had her bags packed. She had one last one, and then she would be finished. She was supposed to go to their house and wait on them after she finished getting ready.

Beth loaded her suitcase and training case in her SUV. She would go to the post office on her way to their place. She made one last trip into the house then set the alarm and locked the door. She never made it to the Pathfinder. Something pricked her hip, and then she was floating. She couldn't work her arms or legs. She fought to stay awake. What was happening to her?

She looked up into the faces of the Masters and promptly passed out.

* * * *

Mac made it home first by the looks of it. He was disappointed that Beth's Pathfinder wasn't in the drive. She had assured them she would be there before them. She only had two errands to run. Unease drifted down through his mind, but he dismissed it. She was known for being late. She got caught up in writing and would forget the time.

Maybe she had gotten a great idea for another book and was pounding it out while she could remember it.

Mac pulled his phone off his belt and pushed one for her number. It rang and eventually went to voice mail. He frowned and did it again. Once again it went to voice mail. He pressed two, and Mason answered.

"What's up? I'm on my way out of the office now."

"Beth isn't here, and she's not answering her phone. Want to swing by her place on the way home and check on her?"

"Got it covered. I'll call you when I get there."

Mac snapped his phone back on his belt and headed inside. He didn't bother changing clothes. Something in his gut said he didn't need to. He hated it when his gut spoke. It was never wrong.

Ten minutes later, his phone rang. Even the ring sounded ominous. He answered it.

"She's not here. Her purse is in the SUV, but her house is locked up with the security set. I used our key and searched it. She disappeared between the house and the Pathfinder."

"Fuck! I'm on my way."

He didn't bother putting the phone back on his belt. He called the office and requested that Silas and Jace meet him at her house. The two men would know how to process the area. The next call he made was to the hospital where Larry was temporarily housed to find out if he'd gotten away. No, they assured him that the prisoner was locked up tight in their psych area.

He cursed. They'd screwed up. Her stalker hadn't been Larry at all. He'd been telling the truth that he hadn't done any of the stuff they accused him of.

When Mac had sat through his interrogation once they had him behind bars, he had been insistent that he was not guilty of all of the stalking and phone calls. He said that he'd only just found her several days before he was caught. He swore he hadn't planted anything in her house and hadn't been watching her all that time. Mac hadn't believed him at the time. Of course he would lie about it. Now he wasn't so sure they'd arrested the right man.

Who in the hell had her?

He pulled into her drive minutes later. Mason met him as he climbed out of the truck.

"I have Silas and Jace coming to process the area. I checked on Larry, and he's still locked up tight. It wasn't Larry all along. Someone else was the stalker."

"How are we going to find her?"

"I don't know, but we will."

His deputies pulled up and climbed out of their SUV, carrying their gear. Mac directed them and studied the place himself.

Footprints, but they're so scrambled, I'm not sure how we can cast them," Silas said. "We've got a clear tire mark that's not any of the trucks here and not hers."

"Good. I'm going back to the office to go over the evidence again. Let me know if you find anything."

"Follow me, Mason." Mac raced to the truck and climbed in the cab.

He raced toward the office. Urgency spurred him faster. Looking in his rearview mirror assured him that Mason was keeping up.

He pulled into the parking lot of the office and jumped out of the truck almost before he even had it in park. He slammed through the door and ran to the evidence room to go back over everything to see if he could come up with anything new.

Mason joined him, and together they searched until Silas and Jace walked in two hours later. They shook their heads at Mac's silent question.

"Just the tire mark. We got a cast of it. If you can find the vehicle that made it, we can match it. We'll start trying to narrow down what sort of cars use these tires."

"Thanks, guys.

Connie walked in and cleared her throat.

"Is there anything I can do? What's going on?"

"I don't think so, Connie. Beth is missing."

"I thought you already caught the stalker."

"We obviously got the wrong guy."

"Oh." She stepped back at his harsh sarcasm.

Mac sighed and ran a hand over his face. He was scaring her.

"T–There's messages on your desk."

"I can't bother with them right now, Connie."

"Right. Sorry." She turned and walked out.

"You were a little hard on her, Mac."

"I'm too pissed off to worry about that right now."

"Let's go to your office and walk through everything."

Mac drew in a deep breath and nodded. They walked into his office, and Mason took a chair across from Mac's behind the desk.

"We know she had a Peeping Tom a while back, and then a week later, she got the basket with the props from her latest book."

"I don't see where this is going to help us find her. We've been over and over it for the last two hours."

Mac absently went through the messages. There were phone calls from members of the community with suggestions and requests. The mayor wanted to meet next week sometime, and a women's group wanted him to speak on crimes against women. He came across a message from the Quiet Hands Hospital saying they had notified Henry Williams of Larry's discharge.

Figures they wouldn't tell her. He continued reading through the messages as Mason went over the facts surrounding her disappearance.

All he could think about was that time was slipping away. They didn't have a clue who had her. He knew the odds of her coming out unharmed were dwindling as he sat there. The odds of her being alive were getting worse by the hour. He'd never forgive himself if anything happened to her. Mason was covering up the fact that he was already devastated by working in lawyer mode. If they lost her, too…

* * * *

Beth slowly woke up. She kept her eyes closed in case someone was watching her. She tried to keep her breathing deep and slow, but panic worked against her. She felt a little sick to her stomach from whatever they had given her she was sure. She tested her arms and legs and found that she was strapped onto a table of some kind. She couldn't budge the restraints.

Why where they doing this to her? She'd always been good. She hadn't rebelled like many of her old friends. They were always getting into trouble and having to be punished.

She remembered that they had wanted her to move in with them and be their bottom. She hadn't wanted to. She didn't feel that way about them. They obviously hadn't changed their minds. What were they going to do with her? They couldn't keep her against her will forever. Could they?

A sound to her left shot her heart into overdrive. She was almost at the point of panting. When the sound came again only closer, she knew what it was, the single tail. The noise was someone throwing it just short of a snap. The whoosh of air near her had her jerking against her restraints. They would know she was awake now. She opened her eyes.

Light blinded her for a few seconds. Then she could see and realized she was in a basement somewhere, probably below their home. She looked toward the sound of the whip and stared into the eyes of Henry Williams. Martin was nowhere to be seen.

"You're awake, good. I was a little worried that Martin had given you too much."

"Why are you doing this, Henry?"

"Master!" He cracked the whip close to her hip.

"Master. Why?"

"Because you belong to us. We know what you need and can give it to you. You've been living as if you don't need the life you were living while you were here."

"I'm fine without it. I don't need it to be happy."

"You're just deluding yourself. That's why you write those books. You're trying to use them as a surrogate for what you really want."

It was so close to the truth that she felt a sob threatening to escape. She did miss the bondage, the little bite of pain that got her where she needed to be to relieve the pressure. Only now, she'd found Mac and Mason. They could give her what she wanted. She didn't dare say that to Henry. It would only make him angry. She didn't want him angry.

"Please, let me go. I don't want to be here."

"You will soon enough, Beth. You will soon enough. As soon as Martin returns, we will start your training."

She panicked for real now and struggled with her restraints. She pulled and moved until she felt sweat run down her hands. She didn't want to know what they had in store for her. They had always been a little harsh in their training.

"I don't want to go through training. I have the right to say no. I'm using my safe word, Master. Cat."

"Beth, there is no safe word here. You gave that privilege up when you left us."

"But I had to move, Hen—Master. I couldn't stay here after what happened."

"We truly regret that. We made a gross miscalculation. We didn't think the drug we gave him would affect him so severely. We just wanted him to get a little out of hand, so that you would come to us."

"You made him go crazy? You're sick! How could you?"

"Be quiet. I'm going to gag you now. You're entirely too talkative for our new slave."

He forced a ball gag in her mouth and fastened it behind her head. Beth screamed, but it did little good. She could only make moaning sounds. She was scared she would get sick from the medicine and choke on her own vomit. She tried to think about other things, but it didn't help.

She focused on struggling to try and work the table over so that she could at least stand on her feet. Her hands were beginning to go numb. She wasn't going to be able to feel them soon. She struggled harder.

Time passed, and she heard the scrape of a door then footsteps—two sets. Martin was back. The next thing she saw was Martin's face over hers. His grin wasn't sane. She whimpered.

"Hi there, Beth. We are going to have so much fun. You'll soon obey us as you should."

He unfastened her restraints and blood rushed into her hands and feet, causing them to burn and tingle. She cried out behind the gag.

"Let's get you on something a little more comfortable." He threw her over his shoulder and carried her across the room.

Henry was waiting on them and helped him fasten her to the Saint Andrew's cross. They tightened the ties until she thought she would scream. Then they stood back to look at her.

"She still has her clothes on. They have to come off." He produced a pair of scissors and began to cut them off.

Before long, she was naked and scared. While they conversed, she tried to rein in her terror with thoughts of Mac and Mason. They would be looking for her. They would find her. They had to find her.

"We think that you should hang there and contemplate your errors, Beth. We'll be back to discuss your punishments." The two men left her closing the door after turning off the light.

The darkness pushed in on her in a suffocating blanket. She fought back the fear and took slow deep breaths through her nose to clear her head. She couldn't dwell on the possibilities of what they would do to her. Instead, she needed to think of ways to escape. Never mind that it seemed hopeless. There had to be a way.

Chapter Twenty

Mac and Mason were still at the office at nine that night. They were worn out from worry to the point that they were snapping at each other. Nothing they had come up with had panned out. They knew from the tire tracks they were looking for late model sedan, but not much else.

"Why won't the FBI get involved?" Mason asked.

"Because there's no evidence that she's been taken across the state line. We don't even know which fucking direction to look."

They finally went home around midnight, exhausted and heavy hearted. They drank a beer before heading off to bed. Mac took a shower and then lay in bed unable to sleep. Random thoughts kept popping in and out of his head. He couldn't figure out why his messages kept intruding into his thoughts about Beth. Then his mind focused on one of the messages. There had been a note about Quiet Hands having notified Henry Williams of Larry's discharge. She had kept in touch with him from time to time. Why hadn't he notified her?

It hit him. He hadn't notified her because he was the stalker and had used Larry's being let out as a smoke screen for his activities surrounding Beth. What was it that Henry and Martin did for a living? He racked his brain until he remembered. They owned an electronics store. Bingo! Henry was the stalker.

Mac jumped out of bed and raced to Mason's room. He burst in, startling Mason so that he jumped up from the bed.

"What in the hell is wrong with you?"

"I know who has her. Get dressed. We've got to get to Dallas as soon as possible."

"Who has her?"

Mac hesitated to tell him. Then he sighed. Mason was a grown man.

"Henry Williams."

"No! Why in the hell would you think that rat bastard has her?"

"That message on my desk. He was the one notified that Larry was released. He didn't inform her. Why? Because he planned to use his discharge as a smoke screen for him stalking and eventually kidnapping her. He hadn't planned on Larry getting caught so soon."

Somewhere during the explanation Mason had begun to get dressed. By the time Mac had finished with his reasoning, Mason was dressed. They hurried out to the truck and climbed in. Mac set a desperate speed using his lights as an emergency vehicle.

They arrived in Dallas less than an hour and forty minutes later. Mac notified the local police department of what was going on and requested backup. They were more than happy to cooperate. They met him a mile from Henry and Martin's house. They went over a plan for getting into the house. The police insisted they had to have a warrant or they couldn't go inside.

"I don't think they are going to admit to having someone against their will and let us in," one of the policemen said.

The police assured the men they had a judge they could persuade to sign the warrant. Precious time was giving out. Mason knew that if she was still alive, and if she was basically unharmed, they were pushing the limit of finding her. If he and Mason hadn't involved the police, they might have been able to beat the information out of them. However, they could easily have not given them what they wanted.

By the time they had the warrant in their hands, Mac was beside himself with fear for her. It had taken entirely too long as far as he was concerned. He'd told them all that in so many words. Mason tried to calm him down, but Mac wasn't going to calm down until they had Beth home safe and sound.

Fortunately the other law enforcement personnel understood Mac's desperate state and didn't hold it against him. They just cautioned him to let them arrest the man once they found evidence of kidnapping. Mac reluctantly agreed, but warned them to get the bastard under lock and key if anything was wrong with Beth.

"I'll beat the man within an inch of his life if you don't get him away from me."

"Easy, Mac. Don't say something you'll regret later."

No doubt Mason was afraid he would threaten to kill the man. As a lawyer, he was protecting Mac or so he thought. Mac didn't need protecting.

"Mason, I don't need you to look out for me."

"Then don't go acting like an idiot."

They approached the house from all sides. At exactly 6:00 a.m., Mac, Mason, and the police burst in through all three doors, the alarm blaring. They quickly cleared the house until they found both men racing to get dressed. Mac penned Henry by the neck to the wall.

"Where is she, you bastard? Where the fuck is she?"

"I don't know what you're talking about. What are you doing in my house? This isn't your jurisdiction, I'm sure. You're from Riverbend. Officer, this man has stalked me and my brother before."

The policemen ignored him and advised him to speak up about where he had the woman. He refused to say a word. Mac began looking for a door somewhere that would lead to a playroom. They had to have one. Most BDSM Masters had one in their homes.

He and Mason searched the house from top to bottom. Then they searched the garage. They had almost admitted defeat when Mac decided to search one more time. He was in the kitchen, opening every door when he walked into the pantry and looked around. After a few minutes of searching in there, he lifted the linoleum off the floor where there was a spot peeled back. There beneath it was a trapdoor.

He called out to the police what he had found and lifted the door. It was pitch-black down there.

"I need a flashlight."

God, if she was down there, she had to be scared half to death in the dark. It had to be pitch black with no windows to allow any sort of light inside.

Someone handed him a flashlight, and he descended the narrow stairs. He shined the light around the immediate area looking for a light switch. He found it on the opposite half wall and switched it on. Light suffused the area. Mason climbed down behind him as they emerged into a short hallway. When they got to the door, it was locked.

"Fuck!" Mac tested the door. It was pretty stable.

"We need the key," Mason called back up the stairs.

Time seemed to stand still as they waited. Mac didn't know how they got the key, but Mason retrieved it from the policemen waiting on the stairs for them to open the door.

Mac unlocked it and burst through it. At first pass, he didn't see her anywhere. Then he spotted her on the St. Andrew's cross and ran toward her.

Fuck, fuck, fuck. Please let her be okay.

Mason took one side while Mac took the other. They unstrapped first her feet, then her hands. Mason took the ball gag from her mouth, and she sobbed and coughed trying to talk.

"Easy, baby. It's okay now. We've got you." Mason took off his shirt and quickly put it around her.

The police emerged into the dungeon shaking their heads at the various apparatuses. One of the men checked out a table with straps attached to it.

"Check her wrists, you guys. There's blood all over these straps over here. If it's not hers, there may be another woman down here."

"Aw, hell. Look at her wrists, Mason. They're rubbed raw."

"Her ankles are the same way."

Mac called out that it was probably hers. Beth nodded and looked away from Mac.

"It's okay, baby. You're fine now. Whatever happened, we'll make it okay."

"I want to go home, Mac. Please take me home."

"Baby, these men have to have a statement, and I want you checked out at the hospital."

"No, Mac, I don't want to go to the hospital. Can't you take me back to Riverbend? The doctor there will take care of me. Please, Mason."

Mac looked at Mason. He knew his brother would do anything for her. In this instance, he was with Beth. She could get checked out at home. Still, she had to give a statement.

"Just give them a statement here, and then we'll run back to Dallas for a more in-depth one later."

The police agreed to this and sequestered her in another room in the house to give her statement. Mac waited impatiently for her to finish. It seemed to take forever, and he didn't like that she was all alone with strange men. Mason had tried to go with her as her counsel, but they didn't buy it.

"What the hell is taking so long?" Mason asked.

Mac watched his brother pace back and forth. They stood outside the room where they had taken her. Both Martin and Henry had been cuffed and taken to the police station. Mac would have to deal with jurisdiction problems later. Right now, all he was interested in was taking care of Beth.

"They have to get her statement from when everything started 'til now. I don't like it, but if we want those two bastards to pay, then she has to do it."

Mason was about to say something else when the door opened and one of the policemen led Beth out toward them. Mason and Mac covered the distance between them in a split second.

"Let's get you home, baby." Mason picked her up.

Mac led the way to unlock the truck doors. He helped Mason get her inside then ran around the front of the truck to climb into the cab.

Once inside, he started the truck and pulled back on the road to head home.

Beth buried her head in Mason's shoulder for the entire drive back to Riverbend. He called her doctor and had him meet them at the local hospital. Beth didn't even protest that. Mac was extremely worried about her state of mind. She'd been through so much already. What little trust they had built up with her was going to be impacted by this. Two men she'd trusted more than anything had betrayed her once again. Mason looked over at him. He was obviously thinking along the same lines.

Mac pulled the truck up to the emergency room. Mason jumped out and ran to get someone with a wheelchair. Mac climbed out of the cab and ran around to lift her out of the truck and settle her in the wheelchair. Mason waved him on so he resigned himself to having to park the truck. It took him less than five minutes to park and make it back to the emergency room doors.

A receptionist caught him before he made it through the door.

"Sheriff, we need information on her. Can you help me so we can make sure they have her records?"

Mac cursed but stopped and helped them fill out her paperwork from what he knew. He realized it wasn't much. He planned to remedy that as soon as they had Beth back to normal again. She was moving in with them one way or another. He couldn't live with something like that happening again. He'd lost at least a year off of his life while she'd been missing.

"Mac. They have her in the exam room and won't let me in there." Mason had his hands in his pockets and was standing outside one of the rooms.

"Is the doctor here yet?"

"I haven't seen him, but he might already have been in the room waiting on her."

"Did she say anything to you before they kicked you out?"

"No. She was still crying though. I'm worried about her, Mac. I hope this hasn't broken her."

"She's strong. She's going to be fine. We'll have a fight on our hands, though. I'm not letting her go back to that house alone. I'll stay with her if I have to."

"We can take turns if we need to until she agrees to live with us."

Mac nodded and stared at the closed exam room door. He willed it to open and someone come out that he could grill for information. Nothing happened for what seemed like hours. Finally, the door opened, and the doctor emerged. He zoomed in on them and motioned them farther away from the room.

"Sheriff, Mason. She's one shaken-up young woman. Physically, she's in fairly good shape. She has some very painful bruising and cuts on her wrists and ankles, but nothing else that I can find. She denies any sort of assault, sexual or otherwise, but she refuses to talk about being upset." He drew in a deep breath and let it out in a huff. "She's going to need counseling. I'll leave the names of several good therapists for her to choose from."

"Thanks, Doc. When can we take her home?" Mac was ready right then.

"Not for another couple of hours. I want to observe her and be sure she doesn't go into shock from the ordeal. I'm giving her something to help her relax. It will make her sleepy, so she can rest some while she's here."

"When can we see her?"

"I take it that you're claiming her."

"Yes, we are."

The doctor sighed and nodded. "I'm not a fan of your threesomes, but I have to admit that you take good care of your women. I'll write the order that you both can stay with her as long as it doesn't upset her."

"Thanks, Doc." Mac shook the man's hand.

Mason did the same then hurried over to the exam room and opened the door to go in. Mac followed right behind him.

They stopped just in the doorway as a nurse held a finger up to her lips to tell them to be quiet. It looked as if Beth was sleeping. They nodded and eased around the room to let the nurse out. She whispered as she walked out the door for them to be quiet and let Beth rest.

Mac rolled a stool over next to the bed and sat down. He watched as Mason picked up a chair and set it on the other side of the bed. Neither man made a sound. They just watched her sleep. She had bandages around her wrists and an IV running from her arm to a bag of something hanging from a pole by the bed.

Several times, she moaned and moved her head back and forth on the pillow, but she didn't wake up. Mac was unsure if he should touch her and try to comfort her or let her alone. He felt helpless and didn't like that feeling one bit. Looking over at Mason, he could tell his brother felt the same way.

A nurse drifted in and out several times checking her and the IV over the next two hours. Finally, Beth opened her eyes. Mac saw her first and smiled down at her. She just stared up at him without changing her expression. Mason and Mac exchanged looks. She wasn't responding to them. This wasn't good.

"Beth, baby. Can you hear me?"

She didn't acknowledge them at first, but then she looked up at him. Her eyes were watery, but she wasn't crying.

"Everything is going to be okay now. No one is going to hurt you again." Mac tried to stay calm talking to her. Emotion threatened to overwhelm him, though.

"I want to go home, Mac."

"I'll get the doctor," Mason said and stood up.

"We'll go home, baby. Let Mason get the doctor to discharge you."

"Okay." She closed her eyes.

Mason hurried out of the room, leaving Mac to watch over her. She looked so frail lying there on the stretcher. He hated seeing her like that. When they got her home, they would tend to her. She needed some pampering. A tub bath was out, but they could give her a massage and treat her with her favorite food.

Mason returned with the doctor in tow. Mac stepped out of the way as the doctor stepped up to the bed.

"Beth? Are you ready to go home?"

She opened her eyes and nodded. "I want to go home now."

"How are you feeling?"

"I'm tired, and my wrists hurt, but I'm okay."

"Okay. I want to see you back in the office on Monday to look at those sore places on your wrists and ankles."

"Okay." She nodded her head a few too many times.

Mac wanted to gather her up in his arms and shield her from the world. He couldn't stand to see her so defeated looking.

The doctor turned to Mac and Mason. "I'm going to write her discharge papers up. I'm giving her a mild sleeping pill to help her rest if she has trouble at night. It would be good if she could talk about her ordeal. If she won't talk to you, get her one of the counselors I'm going to write down on her paperwork."

"We'll take care of it, Doc. Thanks," Mac said.

The physician left them there. A nurse walked in right behind him and gave them a pair of hospital scrubs for Beth to wear home.

Mac held them up. They would be too long, but other than that, they would fit well enough.

"Let's get you dressed, baby."

Mac helped her sit up. Then he opened the gown and pulled the sweat top over her head. He helped her down, being careful of her IV. Mason helped her slip the pants on and tie the drawstrings. All they need now was for the nurse to come and disconnect the IV so that her arm could go through the arm hole.

Finally the nurse appeared and removed the IV. Then she went over the discharge paperwork with Mac and Mason. Beth wasn't paying attention at all. She was busy checking out the ties and uniform she found herself wearing.

As soon as they finished the discharge paperwork, Mac went and got the truck. When he pulled around to the outpatient entrance next to the emergency room, Mason helped Beth out of the wheelchair and into the truck. She was a little more responsive this time. Getting to go home had animated her a little more.

After Mason buckled her in, Mac pulled out of the drive and headed home. They had taken her bags to their house earlier, so she would have clothes to wear. There was no way they were taking her back to her house. He hoped they wouldn't have a fight on their hands.

Chapter Twenty-One

Beth looked up when Mac parked the truck. They weren't at her house. Why was she not surprised?

"This isn't my house."

"I know, but you can't stay there, Beth."

"Why not?'

"Because you don't need to sleep on that fucking couch again."

"Mac," Mason cautioned.

"Baby, you're not going to be comfortable there. You haven't been since finding out someone had bugged it. Stay with us until you can decide what you are going to do." Mac looked desperate.

Beth sighed. What choice did she have right now? He was right. She wasn't comfortable in her own home anymore. She supposed she was going to have to sell the house and find another place to start over. She loved her little house.

"Okay. Just until I figure out what I'm going to do."

Both Mac and Mason let out a breath. It was obvious that they were relieved that she had agreed to stay with them.

"I have everything that was in your car already at the house. Is there anything else you want? Maybe your computer?" Mason asked.

"I do want my computer and my jump drives. They're in a case next to my computer."

"I'll go get them as soon as we have you settled in."

Mac opened the door to the house. Mason followed, carrying her inside. He wouldn't let her walk. He didn't want her putting pressure on her ankles yet.

Mason kept going through the living room and up the stairs to the bedroom. Only then did he put her down—on the bed. She sighed. They were going to baby her the entire time she was there. But then, maybe that wasn't entirely a bad thing. She was shaky from the entire ordeal.

"Let's get your clothes off and put you to bed for a nap. This has been a long day for you." Mason began pulling off the scrubs.

"It's only three, Mason."

"You need more sleep. I'll lie down with you if you want."

"I don't know." She wasn't sure about that. Would she freak out if he did?

"Let's get you in bed first, then."

Once she was under the covers, he pulled off his shoes and stretched out on top of the covers next to her. He rolled over and gave her a quick peck before returning to his back. Beth decided that it wasn't so bad since he still had his clothes on.

Thirty minutes later, she still wasn't asleep, but she was more relaxed. Maybe lying down hadn't been such a bad idea. She no longer felt like things were closing in around her. The idea of sleeping in the dark gave her the willies, though. She might have to have the bathroom light on like a little kid.

Her mind raced around in circles, stopping at random places. Like what did Mac and Mason see in her? She wasn't anything special. What was she going to do about it? She wasn't sure how she could bear to give them up. She loved them, but they were Dom Masters. She didn't think she could go back to that again. Especially after what Martin and Henry had done.

Maybe it all came down to trust. Did she trust them enough to be what they wanted? They had more than lived up to what she wanted. They were kind, caring, intense at times, and insistent that they loved her. Since she loved them, could she ask them to give up what they had known for most of their entire adult life?

How fair was she being to them? They had done nothing but coddle to her needs for the last few days. What had she really done for them?

"Can't sleep?" Mason turned over to face her.

"No. My mind won't stop spinning. I can't even get one thought in my head for more than a few seconds. So I'm not solving anything, just winding myself into a mess."

"It's been nearly an hour now. Let's get up and we'll get you something to eat and drink. You're bound to be hungry."

"I don't want to mess up my dinner."

"Nothing heavy then. How about a piece of fruit?"

"That actually sounds good."

Beth started to climb out of bed before she remembered that she didn't have any clothes on.

"Where are my clothes?"

"Oh, sorry. I unpacked them and put them in the dresser. You can rearrange them however you like. I just stuck them somewhere."

"I'm sure it's fine."

Beth rummaged around in the drawers and found underwear, socks, and a blouse. She found her slacks in the closet. She quickly dressed as Mason pulled on his shoes. They descended the stairs together with Mason fussing the entire way because she wouldn't let him carry her. Her ankles did hurt a little, but not enough to warrant being carried like an invalid.

"You're up already," Mac said. "Did you sleep well?"

"I slept fine, but she didn't sleep at all I don't think." Mason shook his head.

"Is there something I can do or give you that would help, Beth?" Mac's worry carried over in his speech.

"No, I just think I'm rested after whatever the doctor gave me at the hospital earlier. Don't worry about me, Mac. I'm fine."

"How are your wounds feeling? Do you need something for pain?"

"No they don't really hurt right now. They're sore more than anything."

"Do you want to sit on the couch and watch TV?"

"That would be nice." She sat on the couch and rested her feet on Mac's lap.

"I'm going to go get your computer and things. I'll be back in a few minutes." Mason kissed her on the top of the head before leaving.

"What do you want to watch?"

"Anything, just something to make noise I guess."

Mac searched around and settled on a documentary on some wild cat or another. She halfway watched it but was still thinking about their relationship. It was off to a rocky start that was nobody's fault outside of Henry and Martin. She shivered. She still couldn't believe that they had been the ones behind all of her problems. And bugging her house? That had been by far the worst thing outside of kidnapping her. Now she didn't feel comfortable there at all.

The boring show soon put her to sleep and into a dream about the three of them living happily in Riverbend.

* * * *

Mason returned about forty minutes later with a truckload of things. He had brought her computer and all the things around it on the desk as well as some books that were lying around. It looked like she'd been reading through them. By the time he had it all loaded, the time had slipped away with him.

He found Mac on the couch with Beth's feet in his lap. She was fast asleep. He had to smile at the little snoring noises she made.

"I brought back everything I thought she might like. I'm going to unload it."

"Need my help?" Mac started to get up.

"No, you stay with her. It won't take me long. I'll put the computer and supplies in the dining room for now since that is where she was before."

"Good idea," Mac said.

Mason walked back outside and began unloading the truck. He set up her office on the dining room table and thought about where they could make an office for her in the house. There was the spare room behind the kitchen. Right now it housed their junk. It would be perfect for her a place. It was private, close to the kitchen, and secure.

When he returned to the living room, Beth was awake again. They were watching something on the Discovery Channel. He watched them for a few minutes, thinking that they looked good like that. She looked good in their home. Now if they could just convince her to stay.

"I have everything set up for you in the dining room, baby. You can write whenever you feel like it. Do you already have something started?"

Beth turned and looked up at him with a tentative smile.

"Thanks, Mason. I have something started, but I haven't worked on it in a month. I will have to get back into it."

"Hey, Mac. Can you come help me with something real quick?"

Mac lifted his eyebrows but lifted Beth's feet off his lap and gently laid them down on a cushion when he got up. He followed him into the kitchen. Mason continued on into the back room.

"What are we doing in here?"

"What do you think about making this Beth's office?"

Mac's face broke out into a giant grin. "I think it's perfect. We need to clear it out then talk to her about what her dream office would be to get an idea of colors and such."

"That's right. It can be a surprise for her."

"How are we going to get it done without her knowing about it?"

"We'll think of something. In the meantime, let's move a few things out here and there to get ready."

"You talk her up about what she wants in an office. You're better than I am about that kind of thing." Mac followed Mason as he returned to the kitchen.

They each got a beer and walked into the living room to find that Beth wasn't where they had left her. Mason knew Mac was about to panic.

"Check the dining room. I bet that's where she is."

They looked in the dining room and sure enough, she was in there pecking away on her computer. They backed out and grinned. It was the perfect time to move a few things out of that room. Mac and Mason spent the next hour relocating their things. When they called it quits, they only had a few things left to deal with. They felt good about it.

Mason checked in on Beth. She was still working. It amazed him how she could spend all that time in front of the computer and get lost to the world around her. He knew they had made all sorts of noises, yet she hadn't once come to check them out or acted like they had bothered her.

"I'll start dinner. You check and see if she wants something to drink." Mason pulled out ingredients to make spaghetti.

He was on top of the world as he cooked their dinner. Mac returned with a sheepish look on his face.

"What?"

"She fussed at me for startling her. All I did was walk in the room and clear my throat to ask her, and she jumped."

Mason frowned but just shook his head. "So, did she want something?"

"Yeah, I'll get it."

Mason watched him pull out a beer and pop the top. He carried it in the other room. When Mac returned, he grabbed a beer for himself and handed him one. He popped the top and took a pull on it before setting it down on the bar.

"How long 'til dinner?" Mac asked.

"Another forty-five minutes. The sauce has to simmer, and then the bread has to bake. What did you need to do?"

"I want to check in with the police and see what is going on with the case. I really think we should have jurisdiction, but you know, as long as the bastards are under lock and key, I don't rightly give a damn."

"I agree. I plan to talk to the state district attorney about the case myself. I want to be sure they get the maximum possible."

A sound alerted them that Beth was walking in. They both looked up as she entered the room. She looked at them and frowned.

"Did I interrupt something?"

"No, baby. Come on in. We're talking about planning the trip for next weekend since we missed out this weekend."

"Oh, I don't know. I mean, I don't know where I'll be next weekend."

"Right here with us," Mac said.

She frowned and drew in a deep breath. Mason hurried to smooth it over.

"We want you to stay with us while you're deciding what to do. I don't think you can go back to your house. You stiffen up every time you think about it or we bring up something about it.

"Well, I can't just live with you guys."

"Why not?" Mac began. "You know how we feel. We want you to live with us. We want you for always, Beth."

Mason walked around the bar to her. He pulled her into his arms and ran his hand up and down her back in a soothing motion.

"Why not move in with us and see how it goes. If you decide you can't handle it, then you can find another home, and we'll help you move in. You can sell your house in the meantime and put the money in savings until you figure out what you're going to do." Mason held his breath.

"Let me think about it. So much has happened. I'm scared to commit to anything right now."

"Baby, we love you. We'll support you no matter what, but remember, we're going to try and convince you to stay. We'd be foolish not to." Mac reached out and tapped her nose with his finger.

* * * *

"I came in to ask you something."

"What?" they both asked together.

"Can one of you drive me over to the house so I can pick up a few things that I need?"

"I missed something." Mason sighed.

"It wasn't your fault. I didn't tell you to get anything but my computer and jump drives. You even brought most of my desk with you." She smirked at him.

"I'll take you now, baby. Mason said it would be a while before dinner is ready anyway. Do you need anything before we go?"

"No, I'm ready when you are."

Mac ushered her out to the truck and helped her in before closing the door. She had already fastened her seat belt by the time he made it up in the cab. It took all of three minutes to make it to her house. After helping her back down, they walked up to the house, and Mac opened the door for her. She disarmed the security system and they went inside.

"Where are we going?"

"To my office. I need a few things from in there."

She chuckled when she walked into the room.

"What's so funny?"

"Mason did just about empty the top of my desk when he brought things over."

"He wanted to make sure he had everything you needed."

"He pretty much got everything, too. I just need some research material since this is a new book."

Mac grinned. "What kind of research material?

She rolled her eyes at him. "Not that kind. I think someone already confiscated some of *that* kind."

Beth dug through her files and found the folders she wanted. She piled them on the table then reached inside her desk drawer and pulled out a notebook. She added it to the pile on the table.

"That's about it."

"Why not pack another suitcase of clothes while you're here so you don't have to come back very soon. You're going to stay for a while, so you need more clothes."

Beth couldn't fight his logic. She shrugged and walked over to the bedroom and pulled out a suitcase. While she packed more clothes, Mac took her files out to the truck. Once she was finished, he carried her suitcase, and they locked up the house. On the way back to his house, Beth wondered why she hadn't felt bad about leaving her house. Maybe it was because she had already sold it in her head. That settled it. She was going to sell the house. She would list it on Monday.

"What are you smiling about over there?" Mac glanced her way before watching the road.

"I made a decision. I'm going to put the house up for sale tomorrow. You're right. I can't bear to stay there anymore. Are you sure you don't mind if I stay with you for a while until I find another place to live?"

"I've already told you. We want you to live with us permanently. You're welcome there. We would like it if you would consider it your home instead of looking elsewhere."

"I've got to think about it, Mac. I'm confused right now. I need time to figure things out again."

"Fair enough. Just don't go buying a house that you aren't sure about. Take your time, and pick one that's right for you."

"I won't jump into anything. That includes living with you two." She smiled to soften the words.

He didn't reply. They pulled into the drive, and he jumped out to help her down. She pulled out her files before he could stop her. She could take something in, and his hands were busy with her suitcase.

The aroma of Italian herbs and spices filled the kitchen when she walked inside. It felt good to be there. It felt like she was coming home.

I have to stop thinking about it like that. I may not stick around, and pinning emotion on this place will only make it that much harder to leave when the time comes.

She dropped the file folders and the notebook on the dining room table next to her other things then wandered back into the kitchen where Mason was putting the bread in the oven. He turned around and smiled at her.

"Hey there. Once the bread is done, we can eat. Give me fifteen minutes."

"I'm good."

"Do you miss your office? I'm sure working off our dining room table isn't ideal."

"It's fine for now. My office at home wasn't perfect, but it worked for me."

"If you could have your office any way you wanted it, what would it be like?"

"That's easy. I've drawn my dream office off and on for years. I kept saying I was going have it done at my house, but never got around to it."

"Where are the plans? Do you have them here?"

"Yeah. Come on, and I'll show you."

She led the way back into the other room. Mason pulled up a chair as she dug through her office things and pulled out a small folder. She opened it and pulled out several sets of plans that she'd drawn. Mason took them and studied them. He nodded and handed them back.

"What colors were you thinking?"

"I want lime green walls and oak-stained wood for the shelves. I like hardwood floors, but it would depend on if I could afford to have them put down or not. I can always do it later."

"You've really put a lot of thought into it. You know, if you moved in here with us, we could build your dream office for you."

"You're trying to bribe me, Mason." She narrowed her eyes at him.

"Whatever works, baby. Whatever works."

"I bet the bread is ready."

"You're probably right. I'll go take care of that. You find Mac, and drag him to the kitchen so we can eat."

Chapter Twenty-Two

Beth was quiet during dinner. She was too busy thinking about Mason's offer to build her dream office. He wasn't playing fair. That office had been a dream of hers for years. Even before she was writing, she'd wanted it for her editing job. Now he was literally handing it to her on a silver platter. The only catch was that she had to live with them. As bribes went, it was a doozy.

"You're not saying much. Is the spaghetti okay?" Mason asked with concern in his eyes.

"It's delicious. I'm just thinking. I'm always like this when I start a new book."

"Okay, we won't interrupt your thoughts then." Mason grinned at her.

Mac shook his head and leaned over toward her. She leaned closer to hear what he was going to say. Instead of saying anything, he kissed her lightly on the lips. It startled her. She wasn't expecting it, and it hadn't bothered her. Well, it had bothered her, but not in a bad way.

"What's the name of your next book?" Mac asked.

"I don't have a name yet. I usually name my books once they're over halfway finished."

"Is it BDSM or something different?"

She shivered. Just the mention of that bothered her now. She wondered if she would ever be able to write it again. It had been one of her best sellers.

"No, it's a ménage book."

"Now that sounds interesting," Mason said, wiggling his eyebrows.

"Pervert!"

"Look who's talking? It's the woman who writes about it."

Mac pushed his plate away and leaned back on the barstool. She watched his expression as she licked her lips. His eyes grew darker, and he sat up straighter. When she looked at Mason, he was doing the same thing. She realized that despite her recent abduction, she was still attracted to both Mason and Mac. Her panties had already grown damp just from that kiss from Mac. It had been such an innocent and simple kiss.

"Finished eating, baby?" Mason's voice sounded deeper.

When Mac spoke, it thrummed against her clit.

"We'll clean up the dishes later. Let's go sit on the couch."

She was scared that there would be a wet spot on the barstool when she got up.

Mason walked around the bar and took her hand. Mac took the other one, and they helped her down. Then they escorted her to the couch. They crowded her when they all sat down. She had one on each side of her.

Mac broke the ice by drawing her earlobe into his mouth and stroking it with the tip of his tongue. He sucked on it as Mason licked and nipped along her jawline. She moaned, unable to choose which way to lean. She wanted both of their mouths on her.

"Baby, you're so responsive for us." Mason moved further down her neck until he made it to her shoulder. He moved the blouse aside as she sucked and bit her there.

Mac abandoned her earlobe, leaving it wet and hot in the cooler air of the room. Instead, he focused on her mouth. She could deny him nothing as he sucked her tongue into his mouth. Then he followed hers back to her mouth and fucked in and out over and over again. With Mason at her shoulder and Mac loving her mouth, she didn't stand a chance.

"God, baby. I want you so badly. Say you'll let us love you. We'll make it so good for you." Mac ran his hand over her face and rubbed his thumb across her lips.

"I want you, too. I'm afraid, though, Mac. What if I can't handle it?"

"Then we'd stop. You say the word, and we stop. It's always that way, babe.

"Please, Mac. Make love to me." She reached out to Mason and squeezed his hand.

The men growled and stood up. Mac picked her up and carried her up the stairs. When they got to the bedroom, Mason took her from Mac and laid her on the bed. They began removing her clothes as if they were made of glass. Slow and careful seemed to be their motto for the night as they rolled each piece of her clothing down before pulling it off.

Once she was totally nude, they slipped out of their clothes at a much faster pace. She watched them as their delectable bodies emerged for her eyes to feast on.

"You're both so hot. I could watch you all day long."

"We're yours to do with as you please, Beth." Mason spread his hands and walked over to her. "What do you want, baby?"

She licked her lips and smiled. "I want to suck on both of you at the same time."

Mac walked over to stand next to his brother. Both of their cocks were heavy with purplish cockheads that looked almost angry they were so dark.

Beth knelt on the floor in front of them and took both of their dicks in her hands. She pumped on Mason with her left hand and Mac with her right. Both men threw back their heads and moaned as she squeezed them at the base then worked her hands up their cocks. She pumped them several times before sucking Mac into her mouth. She swirled her tongue around his cockhead then licked him up and down like a sucker.

Mason was next. She pulled off of Mac with a pop and took Mason's thick cock in her mouth. It stretched her lips wide almost to the point of pain. She gently raked her teeth over his dick and was thrilled when he hissed out a breath and hung his head.

"Fuck, baby. Do that again. Yeah."

She swallowed around him while he was deep in her throat. The suction pretty much did him in. He cursed again and pulled out of her mouth.

"Work on Mac. I'm not coming in your mouth. I want in your hot cunt, baby."

"I want your ass, Beth. Are you going to let me take you there?"

She didn't answer Mac. Instead, she took his cock into her mouth until he bumped the back of her throat. Then she swallowed around him, tightening her throat muscles until he was cursing.

"Ah, hell, Beth. That's so fucking good." He pumped in and out of her mouth a few times, and then he withdrew so that the suction of her mouth on his cock popped when released.

"Mason. Get her on the bed. I want to taste her sweet cream."

Mason picked her up and placed her on the bed in the center. She looked down the line of her body to where Mac was sliding on the bed toward her pussy. He pushed her legs farther apart with his broad shoulders. Beth wasn't sure she would ever survive his loving. Then he blew on her pussy and licked her slit. It felt so freaking good to feel his tongue at her pussy lips.

Mason settled at her chest and began sucking her nipple into his mouth. His tongue rasped over it several times before he sucked it tight against the roof of his mouth. His fingers plucked at her other nipple then massaged her breast.

The dual sensations of Mason at her breasts and Mac sucking on her pussy sent chills down her spine while heating up her blood.

Mac entered her cunt with two fingers and began pumping them in and out. It felt so good. But it made her want a cock in her pussy. Two fingers just weren't enough. She needed more. Then he curled them and began stroking over her sweet spot. The sensation traveled to her nipples then jumped to her clit. She couldn't stop shaking as her climax built deep inside of her.

Mason began lightly biting her breasts and nibbling at her nipples. The little painful bites were perfect. They stimulated her clit even more. Fire boiled her blood, and she clamped down on Mac's fingers. He hummed his approval against her pussy as he sucked and licked her closer and closer toward the coming explosion.

Pleasure built to the point that she was sure she would explode. Mason twisted her nipples when Mac sucked on her clit, and she shot into orbit, screaming as she did. She clamped her eyes shut as lightning exploded inside of her. Nothing had prepared her for it. It took her by surprise. It had happened so fast. Then the men were pulling back from her, and Mason pulled on a condom then lay flat on his back and crooked his finger toward her.

Beth panted as she crawled on shaky legs and arms toward him. Straddling him, she lifted up and let him fit his thick dick at her entrance. When she started downward, he pushed upward and lodged deep inside her cunt. She yelled out at the pressure of him forcing his way through tender tissue still swollen from her orgasm.

They each pulled back, and then surged toward each other. Finally, she was fully seated with his cock in her cunt. Her pussy lips where stretched painfully wide to accommodate his considerable girth.

"Lean forward, baby. I'm going to play with you a little and get you ready." Mac gently pressed down on her back until she was flat against Mason's chest. He wrapped his arms around her and rubbed her back.

Mac dropped something cold on her back hole. Then he was massaging it inside her little rosette. He pressed the tip of his finger in and out of her before adding more lube and pushing deeper into her ass. The pressure was bearable and the pain minimal. He popped through the resistant ring and began to pump his finger in and out.

Mason whispered naughty things into her ear. "He's shoving his finger deep inside your ass, baby. He's going to add a finger next. Just think what it's going to feel like when you have his cock in your ass while mine fills your cunt."

Mac added more lube and a second finger. This time it burned a bit more and took more pressure to force their way through the tight ring. When he made it through, she breathed out in relief. Then he began to pump them in and out of her. She breathed through the intense pressure and burning that being stretched there caused.

When he added the third finger, she nearly screamed. The pain was almost more than she could take, but she pushed out and felt them ease past the tight ring. Then he was pumping them slowly in and out. God, it felt like a thick stick in her ass as he stretched her wider.

"You're ready, baby. I'm going to fuck your ass with my cock now. I can't wait to get inside your hot ass."

He pulled his fingers out and added more lube. She was already so slick. She was afraid his cock would just slide around instead of slide inside her. Then he was pressing it at her dark hole. The pressure was more intense than she had remembered. Beth pushed out and panted as he slowly worked his thick cock into her ass. Finally, the head passed through the ring with a small pop. He tunneled deeper inside her until he was balls deep in her ass. She shuddered at the pleasure-pain that was beginning to consume her. She felt like instead of the stick up her ass, she now had a telephone pole there. The difference was immense.

Neither man moved. They just lay there breathing hard. She moaned and felt the itch of need begin to grow out of proportion. She wiggled on them and tried to move, but with two dicks inside her, she was helpless to do anything.

"Move! You've got to move. I can't stand it." She thrashed on them, and Mason held her still before pulling back and surging forward again. Mac did the same until they had a rhythm going where one pushed in while the other pulled out and vice versa.

The pleasure that built deep inside her cunt was unbelievable. It grew and grew until she was sure she would be consumed by it. Nothing she did relieved the incredible pressure that swelled.

"Oh, God! I can't stand it. It's too much!"

"You can take it, baby. It's not too much. Relax and let it go." Mason's voice was strained.

She could hear Mac cursing behind her as he thrust his cock in and out of her ass. He moved in quick jabs, shallow then deep. The uneven sensations had her blood boiling even as her cunt began to spasm around Mason's cock. She knew it was only a matter of seconds before she was going to explode.

Fear fought with excitement. It was unlike anything she'd ever experienced before. The tremendous pressure and feeling were so near suffocation that it scared her as her throat worked to exchange oxygen. Suddenly stars exploded behind her eyes, and a roaring filled her ears like a tornado that thundered through a town. It stormed through her and around her until she knew nothing but the unending pleasure that consumed her. It remade her and then tore her apart only to repeat the process over and over.

She tightened around the two men's cocks until they shouted out and exploded with her. She didn't know what they were feeling, but she was beyond comprehension now. She floated in a sea of tingling awareness.

"Son of a bitch! She fucking squeezed my cock off." Mac slowly pulled out of her ass and then dropped on the edge of the bed breathing hard.

"Fucking unbelievable." Mason held her quaking body against his.

Their sweat intermingled. Little things like that came into focus before the world returned for Beth. She felt Mason's chest hair and heard Mac's pants. Then everything roared back into reason, and she passed out.

Chapter Twenty-Three

Beth came back to reality to the feel of warm water and the scent of vanilla. She opened her eyes and found herself in the huge bathtub with Mason holding her and Mac massaging her feet. She looked around, still dazed and a little unsure of herself. She'd never passed out after sex before.

"Hey, baby. How do you feel?" Mason asked.

"Tingly all over."

"I know what you mean." Mac chuckled. "My balls are still tingling."

"What happened?"

"I think we had an unearthly experience. I know I did." Mason squeezed her lightly before running his hands up and down her arms.

"I've never felt anything close to that before."

"Neither have we, baby," Mason said.

They all three soaked in the tub without talking for the next twenty minutes. Then Mac stood up and stepped out of the tub.

"I think the water is cooling off. We better get out now and dry off."

Mason let Mac lift her to her feet and help her out of the tub. She almost couldn't stand on her own. Her legs were weak and shaky. It had been an otherworldly experience all right. She didn't know how to even begin to describe it, and that was a shame because it would have been perfect for a book.

"Baby, you okay to stand alone while I finish drying off?" Mac asked.

She nodded and held on to the countertop just to be safe. Something told her that she wasn't as strong as she thought she was. The men finished drying off and then helped her into the bedroom. They all three climbed into the bed and collapsed.

Beth was wide awake now. She didn't think she would be able to sleep for anything. Needless to say, the men fell asleep almost as soon as their heads hit the pillow. She grinned. It felt so normal right then. She could see herself lying here in the future while they snored on either side of her.

That thought sobered her. Future? Was she actually thinking about a future with them, a forever future?

Beth needed to get up. She needed air. Being as careful as she could not to disturb the men, she finally made it out of the bed by scooting to the foot of the bed and climbing down. She pulled on one of the men's shirts and buttoned the middle three buttons. Then she pulled on a pair of panties.

Forgoing her slippers, she padded barefoot down the stairs and into the kitchen. She snagged a beer from the fridge. She opened it and carried it into the dining room with her and set it on the coaster before she sat down on the chair. The computer called to her, but she put it off. She needed to think about what had happened earlier. It was too important to put off. Everything sort of fell into place for her during the sex. She could totally see herself with them in years to come.

What scared her though was the lifestyle that they played in. She had embraced it once and loved it. She missed it even now, but was scared to try it again. The pleasure-pain of earlier had brought it all back. The experience had been so close to how she felt during play that she almost thought she'd been in her headspace.

Did she trust them? Surely if she loved them and felt like she belonged with them, then she trusted them. How did she test that trust without freaking out? Beth realized that she was seriously thinking about giving herself over to them. It was a scary feeling, but she knew it was important. They assured her that it didn't matter, but it did. It mattered to her. She didn't want to only live part of her life. She wanted the entire thing. That included BDSM. It included letting her Masters take her where she needed to go.

Beth made up her mind, and a great weight lifted from her shoulders. She felt free and empowered.

Turning on the computer, she jumped into the book and was thrilled when it morphed into something more than it had started out as. A damn had broken, and all of her pent-up needs and feelings flowed through her fingers into the book.

Sometime around dawn, Mac walked into the room wearing nothing but jeans that were still unbuttoned. He sat at the table and waited for her to get to a stopping place. She looked up and smiled at him.

"Morning, baby. I guess you didn't sleep very well."

"I wasn't sleepy. I needed to write."

"Are you okay?"

"I'm better than I've ever been." She stood up and walked around the table to him. She straddled his lap and relaxed into his body.

"You sure feel all right." He seemed to hesitate before he huffed out a breath and pushed her back a little. "Beth, I want to ask you something. I probably should wait, but I can't anymore."

"You can ask me anything, Mac."

"Will you marry me, Beth?"

Of all the things he might have asked. This wasn't one she would have thought of. Her heart soared as her spirit leapt for joy.

"I love you, Mac. I love Mason, too. I can't marry you."

His face fell.

"I have to marry both of you."

He looked deep into her eyes and grinned before dragging her into a heady kiss that rocked her world. He pulled back again to stare at her.

"What?"

"I'm just memorizing this moment. It's the best moment in my life."

He stood up still holding her and swung her around the room before letting her slowly slide down his body.

"Let's go tell Mason. He needs to wake up anyway. It's the first day of the rest of our lives."

She laughed and let Mac drag her upstairs to bounce on the bed. Mason groaned and turned over. He opened one eye and winced at the light.

"What's going on?"

"Mac asked me to marry you."

"He what?" Mason sat up and stared at Mac.

"I asked her to marry me, and she said no. She said she had to marry both of us."

"Well, hot damn!" Mason grabbed her and pulled her down on top of him for a kiss.

"I love you, Mason."

"I love you, baby."

"Can I live with you two for the rest of my life?"

"Silly." Mason hugged her again then rolled over, taking her with him until he was on top of her and eager to please.

"I have some requests, but they will wait till later."

"Baby, you can have anything you want," Mason told her.

"I want forever with the two of you."

"We're yours, Beth. For now and always."

Epilogue

"Where are we, Beth?"

"Green, Master."

Mason set down the paddle and picked up the flogger.

"A count of twenty. Count them out for me, Beth."

He swung the flogger lightly against the back of her thighs. Beth's breathing remained normal.

"One, Master. Thank you, Master."

Again he laid it against her skin, this time on her left ass cheek.

"Two, Master. Thank you, Master."

Slash.

"Three, Master. Thank you, Master."

Slash.

"Four, Master. Thank you, Master."

Again and again the flogger rasped against her ass cheeks, or her thighs. At some point, Mac would take over, and she would be able to tell the difference in their styles. She knew all their little differences by heart because they were etched into her heart.

"Where are we, Beth?"

"Green, Master."

The lines of the St. Andrew's cross were etched in her thoughts as she hung from the apparatus. Mason had double-checked all the straps to be sure they weren't too tight before they had started. He would leave nothing to chance. They always made sure she was taken care of.

It hardly seemed like mere months had passed since she'd accepted that she loved and adored them. She would never want a twenty-four-seven type of lifestyle that some embraced, but she'd happily settled into the one they lived now.

"Nineteen, Master. Thank you, Master."

Slash.

"Twenty, Master. Thank you, Master."

"Where are we, Beth?"

"Green, Master." Her answer was breathy now.

Beth was floating now, ready for the last part of their scene. Mac walked over to her and gave her water from a bottle. She drank it like he said to. Then he touched her face so tenderly. When he stepped back, Mason walked over to her and touched her the same way. Then he stood near her so he could see her face as Mac warmed up.

"For a count of five, Beth. Count for me."

Whoosh, pop.

"One, Master. Thank you, Master.

Whoosh, pop.

"Two, Master. Thank you, Master.

Whoosh, pop.

"Three, Master. Thank you, Master.

"Beth, where are we?" Mason asked.

"Green, Master."

Whoosh, pop.

"Four, Master. Thank you, Master."

Whoosh, pop.

"Five, Master. Thank you, Master."

THE END

WWW.MARLAMONROE.COM

ABOUT THE AUTHOR

Marla Monroe lives in the southern part of the United States. She writes sexy romance from the heart and often puts a twist of suspense in her books. She is a nurse and works in a busy hospital, but finds plenty of time to follow her two passions, ading and writing. You can find her in a bookstore or a library at any given time. Marla would love for you to visit her at her blog at themarlamonroe.blogspot.com and leave a comment, or her email is themarlamonroe@yahoo.com.

For all titles by Marla Monroe, please visit
www.bookstrand.com/marla-monroe

Siren Publishing, Inc.
www.SirenPublishing.com